MEDUSA

MEDUSA

*A Novel of Mystery,
Ecstasy and Strange Horror*

E. H. VISIAK

With an introduction by
AARON WORTH

This edition first published in 2025 by
The British Library
96 Euston Road
London NW1 2DB

Medusa was first published in 1929 by Victor Gollancz Ltd, London.

Introduction © 2025 Aaron Worth
Medusa © 1929 E. H. Visiak, printed with permission of the author's estate.
Volume copyright © 2025 The British Library Board

For product safety information, please visit shop.bl.uk/pages/
british-library-publishing, or the Publishing pages on bl.uk.

Cataloguing in Publication Data
A catalogue record for this publication is available from the British Library

ISBN 978 0 7123 5572 8
e-ISBN 978 0 7123 6819 3

Cover and frontispiece design by Mauricio Villamayor
with illustration by Mag Ruhig
Text design and typesetting by Tetragon, London
Printed in England by CPI Group (UK) Ltd, Croydon, CR0 4YY

CONTENTS

Introduction by Aaron Worth   7

A Note from the Publisher   15

MEDUSA

The Introduction   21

PART I

I   The Author's Childhood   25
II   The Author Brings About His Grandfather's Death   29
III   He Goes to School: The Lamentable Sequel   37
IV   His Acquaintance with Mr. Huxtable   47
V   Strange Mysterious Adventures Before Embarking   55

PART II

VI   The Voyage Commenced   71
VII   The Ghost Scare   78
VIII   Mr. Falconer Provides Obadiah   90
IX   Some Remarkable Adventures: The Author Arrives at Pernambuc   98
X   Violent Strange Behaviour of Obadiah: Pernambuc Described   110

XI	The Author Ashore at Pernambuc	118
XII	Departure from Pernambuc	123
XIII	Mr. Huxtable's Sorrow	126
XIV	Astonishing Mystery of the Pirate Ship	134
XV	Mysterious Writing of the Little Mute Man and Discovery of a Monster	144
XVI	Obadiah's Narrative	153
XVII	Obadiah's Narrative Continued	165
XVIII	Quest for the Rock Pillar: Appearances of Lights in the Sea	177
XIX	Mr. Huxtable's Philosophy	185
XX	The Inexpressible Light	197
XXI	Gorgonian Terror	203
XXII	Mr. Huxtable's Consummation	212

INTRODUCTION

I am not sure that E. H. Visiak's champions—and yes, there have been a few, including several prominent figures in weird fiction and criticism—have done him any favours. I do not refer—not primarily, at least—to Colin Wilson's various prefaces to books by and about Visiak, which tend, at least in my view, to damn his literary achievement with praise both faint and equivocal. (The following paraphrase of Wilson's Visiak introductions *in toto* is only—hand on heart—a *little* unjust: "Lovely chap, Harold. Queer book, *Medusa*. Perhaps you've heard that Harold knew David Lindsay? No? Well, have you ever read Lindsay's *Arcturus*? That, now, *that* was a book indeed...") No, I am thinking instead of well-meaning, enthusiastic advocates of Visiak's work who, in their very eagerness to win for him new readers, may sometimes have helped, quite unintentionally, to give rise to unreasonable, not to say unfair, expectations.

Perhaps most notably, in 1983 Rod Serling's *Twilight Zone Magazine* published a "Fantasy Five-Foot Shelf" comprised of short, best-of-all-time lists of fantasy and horror compiled by Karl Edward Wagner, Thomas M. Disch, T. E. D. Klein and R. S. Hadji. Rather astonishingly, Visiak's obscure 1929 novel appears here not once but twice: Hadji includes it, defensibly enough, alongside such other little-read worthies as Adrian Ross's *The Hole of the Pit*, Eleanor Scott's *Randalls Round* and Violet Hunt's *Tales of the Uneasy*, in the "Neglected Masterpieces of the Macabre" list, calling it "one of the most truly original fantastic novels in the English language." Wagner, on the other hand, disdaining the need for any such pusillanimous qualification as "neglected", boldly declares it to be one of the "13 Best Supernatural Horror Novels", *tout court*, of all time. (Disch and Klein play it safer, calling to muster such familiar names and titles as M. R. James's "Casting the Runes", Algernon Blackwood's "The Willows", Charlotte Perkins Gilman's "The Yellow Wall-Paper" and Henry James's "The Turn of the Screw".) More, Wagner accompanied his selection with such tantalisingly cryptic comments as: "If David Linsday had written *Treasure Island* in the throes of a peyote-induced religious experience… Well, if Coleridge had given Melville a hand on *Moby Dick* after a few pipes of opium…" (Elsewhere he suggested that "John Milton may have popped round on his way home from an opium den to help [Visiak] revise the final draft." I think I see a pattern here.) A few years later, by which time *Medusa* had clambered, all slippery and quivering, up into his "Top Three", Wagner called the novel's titular horror "a soul-eating Cthulhoid entity". Hadji made a similar comparison to H. P. Lovecraft, and not to the American writer's advantage, calling the novel "vaguely reminiscent… of Lovecraft's 'The Call of Cthulhu', but… utterly unlike in spirit. Visiak achieved the terror and wonder, the sense of awe, that Lovecraft could only grasp at."

Well, what's wrong with such enthusiastic, full-throated kudos? Nothing at all, in principle; and (for the record) I am very much in the camp of the—shall we say, unconflicted?—Visiak admirers. And I hope, after reading *Medusa*, that you will be too. But it *is* rather a lot to live up to, isn't it? And for all those years during which the novel was all but inaccessible to the general reader, its myth continued to grow, magnified by its very inaccessibility. The *Twilight Zone* lists, Wagner's especially (which is, I grant, idiosyncratic, and not only in its inclusion of *Medusa*), became the stuff of legend, endlessly copied and pasted around the internet, passed on like esoteric lore, sparking online conversations in hushed tones (so to speak) about where and how a copy might be procured. Because, of course, the very scarcity of such a book is part of its appeal, limning it with a weird glamour. To call something a "Neglected Masterpiece of the Macabre"—or, and this is much the same thing, to label a book which virtually no one has ever heard of as one of the very "Best Supernatural Horror Novels" of all time—well, let's just say that epithets like these have predictable and well-documented effects on readers of weird fiction. And I do mean this species of reader particularly, addicted as we are to the trope of the monstrously rare tome whose mere perusal brings madness and death: *The King in Yellow*, *The Necronomicon*, *Vastarien*. We find ourselves wondering, inevitably, whether such a book might really exist (and if so, where can we get it?). You might as well wave a tattered cape in front of a blood-maddened bull. The point is, I'm not sure that *anything* can live up to that kind of build-up. Nor, I think, is the novel well-served by all the comparisons to Lovecraft. It's true that Hadji, at least, calls *Medusa* "utterly unlike" "Cthulhu" "in spirit"; but as linguist George Lakoff likes to say, "Don't Think of an Elephant!" The damage has already been done. Nonetheless, I give you fair warning: *Medusa* is in no meaningful respect a "Lovecraftian" novel. It is not a prequel, sequel, or otherwise kith or kin to "Cthulhu" except in the broadly homologous sense Hadji suggests ("The Call of Cthulhu" did appear the year before *Medusa*, but I think we must file this under the category of "interesting coincidence").

So what, then, *is* it? First, a few words about its maker, who lived a long life, but a relatively uneventful one, to outward appearances at least. Edward Harold Physick was born in 1878, in Ealing. According to family lore, the Physicks were descended from a Phoenician mariner who had been shipwrecked on the coast of Cornwall. I'm not sure why the legendary ancestor was supposed to be Phoenician rather than Greek, since tradition also held that the family's surname was an Englishing of the Greek *phusikos*, "natural" or "physical". (It is really an occupational name, from the Middle English "phisik(e)", signifying "physician".) Why did Harold choose the name "Visiak" when he took to writing? It is closer to "Visick", a Cornish variant of "Physick". It also contains an echo of "vision", a word of immense importance to his imaginative world and work. But more fundamentally, this slight mutation of the family name may simply have signalled a desire on his part to stake out his own creative territory, given that so many of the male representatives of the family line were already renowned in another field of artistic endeavour, namely sculpture, dating back to the eighteenth century (there are half-a-dozen Physicks listed in the 1954 edition of the *Dictionary of British Sculptors* alone). As a young man of nineteen Visiak (as we will call him here) took up a position as clerk in the Indo-European Telegraph Company, where he worked until his dismissal during World War I for his refusal, as a conscientious objector, to be "badged 'on war service'"—in other words to undertake, as he put it, "war work without danger", a situation compounding, he seemed to feel, betrayal of principle with cowardice. Visiak, brought up before the Military Service Tribunals (five times!), recorded an amusing exchange which showed that the Government had done its research on the fledgling writer:

> "I have discovered," he [the "military representative"] said, fixing me with his eye, "that you have written a book... In that book you have described sea-fighting. I say that you are insincere."

"Do you mean that by describing sea-fighting I was encouraging sea-fighting?"

"Exactly."

"I suppose you have read *Paradise Lost*?"

"Yes, yes—"

"Milton describes devilry. Do you think he meant to encourage devilry?"

"You are—*incorrigible*!"

The book thus entered into evidence, as it were, to impugn its author's credibility was *The Haunted Island*, a fascinating, scientific romance-cum-adventure novel ostensibly intended for a juvenile readership. It was published, along with a volume of verse, *Buccaneer Ballads*, in 1910, and both books were well received. Further poetry collections followed, as well as a school novel (*The War of the Schools*) co-authored with the headmaster of York House School in Hampstead, where Visiak had taught after the war. Then came *Medusa*, whose lack of success greatly discouraged Visiak (as he later recalled: "*The Times* ridiculed my novel *Medusa*, and caused the return by booksellers of hundreds of copies; and Gollancz stopped advertisements"), though he still wrote two more novels in the 1930s, *David Treffry* and *The Shadow of Hamond Layton*. The first of these manuscripts was not published until 1968 when it appeared, with minor alterations, as an autobiography titled *Life's Morning Hour*. (I am indebted to Douglas A. Anderson for this and other pieces of information about Visiak.) This is, by the way, a quite wonderful book which helps to put flesh on the bare bones of Visiak's life, though the revelation that it was originally written as a novel gives one reason to regard it with more scepticism as a source of biographical information than when it was understood to be a memoir. *The Shadow* (with this abbreviated title) finally saw print in one of John Gawsworth's Cyclopean anthologies of thrillers, but Visiak had had enough, and turned to scholarship and criticism. He was considered a serious enough Milton scholar to be chosen to edit the Nonesuch edition of the poet's works, which appeared in 1938.

Encountering the work of Milton had indeed been one of the great transformative experiences of his life, and it is one of *Medusa*'s crucial intertexts—the phrase "Gorgonian Terror", for instance, which is used as the title of the novel's remarkable penultimate chapter, comes from Book II of *Paradise Lost*, in which the classical figure of Medusa is, rather incongruously, placed in Hell, where she prevents the damned from partaking of the oblivion-granting waters of the River Lethe. A second life-changing event, if Visiak's novel-memoir is to be trusted, was his experience of a violently powerful "vision" of the ineffable, the supernal, the inexpressible; he suddenly perceived "great arcs of light indescribably bright", followed by the appearance of a figure "*unimaginable* and, although seen clearly and definitely, indescribably, incomparable with any known form." A firsthand experience, in other words, of the Sublime.

And sublimity, Visiak believed, is a vital, perhaps necessary, ingredient of weird fiction. In his 1936 essay "On the Significance of Horror Fiction", which I take to be an attempt to adapt T. S. Eliot's influential historical argument concerning the dissociation of sensibility in poetry to the context of horror writing, Visiak writes: "There is, in fact, a real relation between horror and sublimity. The faculty of evoking horror in fiction is allied to the power of sublime creation. The one is the other in modified form." So what, then, is *Medusa*? Here is one way to answer that question. Take a child whose formative years were spent immersed in adventure, historical, and "boys'" fiction by Stanley Weyman, Robert Louis Stevenson,

H. Rider Haggard and Jules Verne. Let him then discover the horror-worlds of Poe, Conrad, Melville, Le Fanu and Hawthorne, among others. Let him, further, be transformed utterly by exposure to the works of John Milton, then have his inner world rocked a second time by a quasi-mystical vision of enormous potency (for there is no need, you see, *pace* Wagner, for the involvement of any illicit mind-altering substances in Visiak's creative process). Mix in a wealth of deep and miscellaneous learning, permitting its possessor the ability to construct a seamless stylistic pastiche, and to craft an interpolated philosophical parable or myth reminiscent of Plato, More or Bacon. Then let him attempt a mighty and ambitious "Story of Mystery and Ecstasy and Strange Horror" (the novel's original subtitle). The result, as the great Welsh fantasist Arthur Machen (himself no stranger to the unjust vicissitudes of critical taste) saw, is a nightmare, one in which—but let's let Machen himself have the last word:

> Most people have experienced the unspeakable horror that is called nightmare… For a moment, on awakening, rather, it seems probable, for some fraction of a second that is almost outside of time; one realises the full impact of the overwhelming and shuddering terror that has passed; and then, as the dreamer would realise the vision to himself, he perceives that it is beyond the power of words, nay, beyond the power of thought to express. Certain terrible symbols are all that remain. I think that Mr. Visiak has succeeded in setting down these symbols in his book. "Medusa" is a nightmare: almost recollected.

A NOTE FROM THE PUBLISHER

The original novels and short stories reprinted in the British Library Crime Classics series were written and published in a period ranging, for the most part, from the 1890s to the 1960s. There are many elements of these stories which continue to entertain modern readers; however, in some cases there are also uses of language, instances of stereotyping and some attitudes expressed by narrators or characters which may not be endorsed by the publishing standards of today. We acknowledge therefore that some elements in the works selected for reprinting may continue to make uncomfortable reading for some of our audience. With this series British Library Publishing aims to offer a new readership a chance to read some of the rare books of the British Library's collections in an affordable paperback format, to enjoy their merits and to look back into the world of the twentieth century as portrayed by its writers. It is not possible to separate these stories from the history of their writing and therefore the following novel is presented as it was originally published with six edits to the text and minor edits made for consistency of style and sense. We welcome feedback from our readers, which can be sent to the following address:

> British Library Publishing
> The British Library
> 96 Euston Road
> London, NW1 2DB
> United Kingdom

MEDUSA

Medusa with Gorgonian terror guards
The Ford

MILTON

To

J. Anderson Smith

Literary appreciation is not a mere sense. It is an essential of character, exerting great power. It may be said to cast light that can be felt.

I always found my visits to you, though brief and principally concerned with other matters, particularly stimulating to literary endeavour. That integral *value* for literature which you inspired was reviving and invigorating at times when desire failed, and I had almost abandoned my efforts to decipher the script, restore the sequence, and bridge the *lacunæ* of William Harvell's MS.: which could be done only by projecting the imagination into the atmosphere of those remote regions whence (as I believe) it came into my hands.

E. H. V.
August 1929.

THE INTRODUCTION

Book writing is a notorious toil; but the love of fame drives some men to scour the world for matter, that can find little in their own minds; as those miserable Israelites were forced to make bricks without straw. They are hurried into it (as it should seem) by an impetuous rushing wind, which is but vanity.

I was never sedulous to enter a house of bondage; and, if I had been mindful to my own glory, I had long since written this narrative, not deferred it until old age. And, although it be pleasant in the evening of life to live over again the morn, to enact again past scenes on recollection's lively stage, it were too toilsome an adventure to write 'em out, unless one should be a sort of *Moses* of authorship, whose *eye was not dim, nor his natural force abated.*

It is not vanity, therefore, that moves me to indite (by the help of some notes of writing that I kept) the story of my adventures; and, as to diverting my old age, it is sufficiently regaled already with the mere contemplation of those extraordinary, those unimaginable happenings, passing man's knowledge (which may admonish some to read no further, having no propensity for marvels); but that I would not willingly leave it to perish with me in the grave.

WILL HARVELL
Portishead.

PART I

CHAPTER I

The Author's Childhood

I was born and had my earliest childhood upon the sea, my father being captain of a small barque plying between Bristol and the island of Jamaica in the West Indies, and my mother going along with him in his voyages.

My recollections of my father, which (as I shall relate) were soon abridged, accord well with what I could learn from my grandmother: that he was a man of a gentle and kindly heart and pensive complexion, rather given to melancholiness. He early discovered a liking for the sea in beholding the ships passing by Portishead, where his home was. My grandmother bought him, in this time, a handsome large playboat, little thinking (as she told me) that thereby she was but nursing that desire which grew up with him; so that nothing could content him while he was yet scarce older than a boy, but going to sea. The poor woman endeavoured to have persuaded him from following this design; but my grandfather not only gave it his countenance, but apprenticed my father, as soon as he was old enough, to a master mariner of Bristol; with whom he sailed in a voyage to New Holland.

What reasons moved my grandfather in encouraging my father to go to sea, whether good or ill, I know not, and will not take it upon myself to build a judgment on what he was become, all harsh and crabbed, at the period when (having lost both father and mother) I came to dwell with him in his house at Portishead. I did hear my father named but once in discourse between my grandfather and grandmother, which was in a reproaching comment she made on his sending him to sea, and his answer:

"What" (cried my grandfather), "do you take upon yourself to lift up your wicked complainings against the sea? Did you never read those words of the Psalmist: *They that go down to the sea in ships, that do business in great waters; these see the works of the Lord, and his wonders in the deep.* Hold your peace, woman, and cease to meddle with things that are too high for you!"

But not everyone that doth quote Scripture is truly religious; and I shall leave my readers to judge in my next chapter whether my grandfather was.

My recollections of my mother are enshrined in that sweet age of childhood, life's short Paradise; and her untimely death cast a sadness over my tender years, and made empty my heart with a pining for affection such as my grandmother, for all her kindness to me, was not able to appease.

I principally relate this early period of my life, however, by reason of an experience which befell in my third or fourth year, being my earliest recollection, it is such a surprising apparent harbinger of those lights that I saw in the sea in my voyage with Mr. Huxtable, as I shall relate.

The first scenes of our life are obscure, like the beginnings of the Creation: it was some strange enchanting light that opened the eyes of my perception in the world. By night it happened, during one of my father's voyages (but the situation I know not); whenas, being carried from my bed to the port in the cabin (I suppose, by my mother), with some vehement exhortations to look, I beheld in the water great glistening lights, as bright as the sun, but soft as the moon, and glancing blue and green as a pearl-shell's lustre.

When I was eight years old, my father's ship was in a tempest cast away on the coast of Spain, both my father and mother and all hands perishing in the waves; but I, as by a miracle preserved in the wild sea, was floated safe ashore.

This was in the middle of a dark night; and my recollection of it is not like real occurrences, but as a confused scene, or as a dream, full of darkness and great roarings and wild alarms and stamping of feet and holloing voices, with sudden claps like thunder and terrible violent flaws of wind, in a dull and stunning sound; and of hurryings to and fro, and my mother's voice sometimes wailing and lamenting, and sometimes attempting to have comforted me while I cried continually. Next, of my lying on the shore in thick darkness, and of the sudden bright shining of a lantern that cast a beam upon the wet sand, and of an austere, kindly countenance of a man bent over me, being dressed all in black, and having a strange wide-brimmed hat upon his head; and of his lifting me in his arms and bearing me some way through the darkness; thereafter, of my dwelling with him in a fair, large house that stood shining white in a garden, wherein there were trees bearing fruits that hung like golden globes on the branches, others having great, massy, red glowing blossoms; and, therewithal, a soft cooing of doves for ever sounding in the sunny warm air.

The Spanish priest (for such he was) treated me kindly all the time I abode with him; and, when I wept for my mother, as I did often, he lifted me on his knee and spoke kindly to me with gentle accents that soothed my tears and solaced my sense like music, though I understood not a word.

There was also an ancient woman lived there, that (I suppose) kept house for him, who cared for me. She wore a pair of horn spectacles, and about the girdle of her black dress a string of beads, with a silver cross, that was called (as I learnt afterwards) a rosary. The skin of her face was withered and wrinkled like old parchment, and her hair, that was grey and yellow in patches, was drawn stiffly up in a topknot upon her head. Sometimes she took me into a church; whereof my recollection is all gaudy and confused, and full of delight, with enchanted bright colours and pealing music and fragrant smoky air; with the priests in their stately gay vestments, and chanting choir-boys, and starry coloured lamps and painted images, and tall candles set up solemn and lofty upon the altar in their candlesticks.

While he entertained me in his house, my kind preserver issued enquiries concerning me. How, or by what means, he learnt that I had a grandfather dwelt at Portishead, I know not; but, as soon as he ascertained it (being after I had abode with him some months), he took me to Coruna, bearing me (as I remember) jogging at his back on a mule, and left me aboard a ship which was ready to sail for Bristol, entrusting me in care of the Captain, a worthy man he was acquainted with. He directed him how to convey me to my grandfather's house; whither, after a voyage that I remember but in glimpses, I came safe, and where I was installed, but with a custodian much unlike the gentle priest.

CHAPTER II

The Author Brings About His Grandfather's Death

My grandparents dwelt in a fair, large, elegant house in the Nore Road, Portishead (or *Possett,* as it is called). My grandfather was a scrivener, but retired from his occupation; and, day after day, and pretty well all day long, he sate in his elbow-chair by the window of the parlour, his feet (being much swollen with the gout) propped on a high stool.

He held still lest he should enrage his gout, puffing slowly at his pipe, or charging it anew; whereupon he did put a camomile blossom upon his tobacco from a plate that stood near an old worn Bible, with his big lead tobacco box, on a table by his side. At each several twinge of gout, he did curse vehemently, raging in clouds of tobacco smoke. Between his cursing and raging, he read his Bible, or prayed bitterly for someone that he saw passing in the street.

The air was thick with his tobacco smoke mingled with the sweet fumes of the camomile blossoms, and very warm too; for he always had his fire burning, even in hot summer. The wooden walls of the parlour were painted blue, and the pictures were solemn engravings of battles in the history of Israel. The bookcase was heavy laden with theological volumes, but I never saw him read in any of them, only the Bible. Ribbons of withered black seaweed hung curled and crinkled from the mantelboard for a decoration. The brass clock on the chimney clicked with a harsh sound.

'Twas all dark and gloomy; yet not to me, for childhood is of purer eyes than to behold gloom; beholding dark places in a sort of suffused colour, by the same enchantment, which, in that sweet age, makes bright things to appear more dilated and radiant, shining clear—yea, and more solid too! it being a fallacy, commonly received, that things, or bodies, etherially seen appear vague and diffuse: no, but all the more definite and materially compacted. Some local recollections of that time especially of various flowers and fruits in my grandfather's garden—honey-sweet fragrant sunflowers, and those little berries on bushes with blue dark bloom upon them like grapes—do come wafted over my thoughts, and steal upon my sense, with such delight as cannot be told. Even my memories of my grandfather are void of gloom, though full of dread.

He, indeed, was wont to relate to me, with lively zest, the terrors of the lake burning everlasting with brimstone and with fire; and, when this fell after nightfall, as commonly it did, I went to rest (at least, to bed) all harrowed with fear, with my thoughts working tumultuously in dreadful imaginations.

On one occasion, being on a dismal evening in the month of November, in the midst of his ravings, my grandfather was become really like a fiend. His meagre face contracted, and his high narrow brow appeared to jut and warp in the candlelight. His eyes, peering narrowly at me, shrunk up steely hard and cold in his head. He cast his pipe breaking upon the hearth, and his voice came cracked and shrill. But, while I stood perfectly terrified at his aspect, and at his words (which I forbear to set down), my grandmother interposed.

"How can you speak such things?" cried she, setting her cap and screwing her eyes up, as her habit was when she was agitated. "I would take shame to do it. I would—"

"Hold your tongue, woman!" cried he, cutting her short, yet somewhat shamefaced, too. "You'ld spoil and ruin the boy! I do but speak to his good!"

"The Lord never meant us—'The Lord is loving and of great mercy,'" said she, misquoting plaintively. But he abridged her again.

"Peace!" cried he harshly. "Have I read in my Bible for three-score years, and must I go to school to you to learn what the Lord means? to be admonished by a woman? to be instructed by the inferior vessel? Down, presumption! Perversity, down! Will, bring me my Bible and another pipe!"

I went all on a tremor to the cupboard where he kept his pipes, although I knew that the box was empty, since he had sent me to the inn that very day with his old foul pipes to have them burned white, having delayed until but one remained, and that one lay broken in pieces on the hearth. I pretended to look in the cupboard while I screwed my courage to tell him that none was left. When I told him, he reviled me after a dreadful manner for not having acquainted him before; and, howling as his gout pronged him, he laid hold on his tobacco-box and cast it crash against the wooden wall.

There was laid up in my mind in this time, a pretty large store of Scriptural texts; for I had a very good memory, and besides my reading to my grandfather out of the Bible (in manner as I shall tell you), he used to commence the morning prayers by opening his Bible at a venture, and, after looking up and down the page, with a sharp eye and a bitter fierce visage, did read aloud some few words that he elected in this narrow compass (for he never turned the leaf), whether or no he found such an one as would sort with his extempore prayer; which he uttered after a slow weighty manner, kneeling with his elbows resting on the seat of his chair; my grandmother and I following suit, she kneeling stiffly up upon a red hassock that she kept for the purpose.

But this part of my grandfather's religion was pleasant to me (and very pleasant is it in my recollection) for the state of expectant relish I was in (with a child's pure appetite) for my breakfast, having in my nostrils the delectable savour of the cooking fare.

My grandfather's discourse during breakfast did much belie the earnest accents of his expressions of thanksgiving; for usually 'twas little else but finding fault with the cook—or rather, with my poor grandmother, who carried herself before him with a demeanour of forbearance, ruffled by a sort of querulous aggravation, the most unwisely that she possibly could; which blew the flames of his choler. She knew not how to be perfectly still, nor yet, the other way, to raise such an astonishing great wind as had made him fearful to provoke it more; which I saw actually done on one occasion, and that by a woman—and this a small sickly woman, to boot—being my great-aunt, my grandmother's sister, when she was affronted by my grandfather in a visit to his house. She was perfectly unafraid of him, and, indeed, had never any cause to fear him after.

My intercourse with my grandfather was mostly in the tasks he set me, and in doing his errands across country to neighbouring villages. The tasks were most in reading, and that in the Bible. When I could read proficiently, which was not before my twelfth year, my writing and ciphering went by the board; and for two hours before dinner, and one late afternoon (if there were no errands), I read to him whilst he sat smoking his pipe, muttering to himself, or complaining at twinges of the gout. If I stumbled or but halted over a word, he immediately began to fret (which made my reading worse), exasperating his gout and working himself into a frenzy of rage and pain, ending, as often as not, by snatching the Bible from my hands and dinging it at my head.

His errands, therefore, were the more welcome to me to let me be away from him. Yet had I an exceeding great fear of meeting with an highwayman. Also, I did abhor to be sent to the apothecary in the High Street, being an ancient big burly man, having a high, red, smiling, satirical countenance, and fierce tiger eyes, that affected me with an unspeakable dread.

My grandfather chastised my offences which were commonly by misadventure (for I had never on purpose dared to do anything to affront him) with canings at the hands of his man. In the meantime, while his man caned me, he read a fit lesson from the Bible with slow and solemn emphasis. When he ceased, so did the caning also; but, if he was in an angry temper, both reading and caning were protracted.

But my grandmother was always kind to me, and sometimes interceded for me; which did but make my punishment the worse; so that I besought her, at last, after such an occasion, not to intercede for me any more. However, when my next castigation was about to fall, after having me into the kitchen, she fortified my breeches with a piece of tarpaulin; which served me well at first. But when my grandfather, looking for the evidences of pain, beheld but a blank physiognomy—when the tarpaulin was proof even against a more vigorous dealing—when, finally, that expedient was perceived, I protest I thought my very bones had broke under the blows that did ensue. Also, my grandfather having learnt (I know not how) that I dreaded to fall in with an highwayman, he contrived to delay my errands as late as he might, to the end that I should return through the open country after nightfall. *One of the old school* he called himself, and I am content. My grandmother loved him; my coming to dwell with him was after his heart was warped with some corroding bitterness, of which the effects, working through me, did make me the instrument of his death.

This was when I had dwelt with my grandparents five or six years; and thus it befell:

On an occasion when, being sick, he sent me to that dreadful apothecary to fetch physic, instead of going I filled the bottle at the village pump, taking care not to be descried, absconding myself for such a time as the errand would have taken; for, the appearance of the physic being just like water, the discrepancy was not like to be remarked.

So I brought it to him (I mean the water in the bottle), and, not suspecting anything, he took a dose. He declared next morning that it had done him a deal of good; and, after taking another dose, he set the bottle back in the cupboard.

About six weeks after, complaining of the headache, he hobbled to the cupboard with his stick, and took the bottle from the shelf. But I grew much afraid, apprehending the water by this time must be poisonous. I tried to have uttered a warning; but fear constrained me, and I stood staring like an antic while he raised his cup.

Yet he did not drink; but, having sniffed at it once and twice with a wry face, he set it down on the table.

"Pooh!" said he, blowing. "What's this? The stuff stinks!" and he turned and looked on me.

He stood looking a long time (or so it seemed to me), bowed forward on his stick with his head thrust out, peering at me.

"Whence came this devil's stuff?" said he, at last, in a whispering, hoarse voice. "Did you get it of the apothecary? Tell me!"

"No," said I, with a small, shaking voice, "I was afraid. I filled it at the village pump."

He uttered a dreadful snarling cry. "Ha!" said he, starting forward. His face, that was meagre and sharp, appeared dull like lead; but there was a look in his pale blue eyes that (by how much I can express) struck as baleful lightning to my soul. I had fled from him; but I could not, being perfectly holden with terror. But, as he came at me, on a sudden he staggered and cast his arms abroad, dropping his stick. Pitching heavily head forward, he fell flat down upon his face.

I ran to the door, calling in a panic to my grandmother; who, entering in, and beholding him in such a posture prone on the floor, she sunk down by his side with a wild crying, looked in his face, took his hand, and fell to wailing over and over that he was dead.

But while she acted thus, I, scarce knowing what I did, took the cup and the bottle from the table and went from the parlour, making my way to the garden. I poured the stinking water on a flowerbed, and cleansed the cup and bottle in the water tub.

Many of the townsfolk attended my grandfather's funeral, especially dissenters, and two or three farmers, also, in their long black coats. I, being dressed in my best clothes, which I used to wear at the meeting-house on Sundays, sat beside my grandmother in the chapel, she weeping often, with her pocket-handkerchief to her eyes, but I mute, being constrained with a sort of numb horror.

During the reading of the burial service beside the grave, that dreaded apothecary, who stood near, turned his head, on a sudden, and looked on me with his tiger eyes. No doubt, 'twas by chance; but it gave me, nevertheless, a horrible scare as if it had been an accusation.

For, though the occasion of my grandfather's death, as I learnt after, was an apoplexy, yet my deceitful and disobedient act did bring it to pass; the secret knowledge of which worked on my mind, so that I suffered grievously as only such a phantastically scrupulous child can; and, of nights, in the intervals of my broken slumber, my grandfather came to me, a horrible and venomous ghost, breathing out damnatory texts, and declaring that I should burn in hell fire for ever. One morning following such nightly terrors, as I remember, I thrust my hand into the fire in an agony of anticipation.

I came near to confessing to my grandmother once and twice, yet never did. But she, beholding my misery and persuaded by friends, resolved to send me to an academy for the sons of gentlemen in Bristol; where (as my readers that be not deterred by such a lamentable beginning, shall learn) I became the hand and instrument of another death.

CHAPTER III

He Goes to School: The Lamentable Sequel

On a summer's morning, not many weeks after, I parted from my grandmother, standing dolorous beside the garden path in the bright sunlight; and my dread of going to the academy nigh made me blurt out the secret of my misery that had persuaded her to send me. But my mind was holden in a sort of apathy.

I passed by under the window-lattice whence so often I had seen my grandfather peering forth at me, expecting almost to see him then (although it would scarce have startled me from my dejection), and descended into the road, being followed by my grandmother's page, that bore my portmanteau.

When we were come into the High Street, I saw some of the shopkeepers standing at their doors, and the sight of their familiar persons did but increase my melancholy; so that, on one of them speaking to me, I had much ado to contain my tears. I begun to walk faster; and, on my grandmother's boy loitering, I took my portmanteau from him. I always misliked this boy, with his shambling gait and crafty, pale, prying face; yet now, on this miserable morning, I conceived a kindness for him.

We had not arrived the *White Lion*, where we were to take a postchaise to Bristol, but he begun to loiter again; and, on hearing a noise of laughter behind me, I turned, catching him standing in the midst of some gazing boys, rubbing his fists in his eyes, miming a crybaby. He was older and bigger than I was; yet, being extraordinary strong of my arms, though spare-made, I could easily have chastised him. But I was too much dispirited. When we were come to the inn, however, I would have sent him back to be rid of him. But he protested that my grandmother had charged him to bear me company to the academy; and, supposing she did design this for my good (as she thought it), that I might, in a manner of speaking, cut a figure in the academy, I did let him go with me, and we mounted into the postchaise.

In this period I should not have minded, but rather have welcomed, an highwayman; but nothing remarkable fell out on the road. We arrived at Bristol about five of the clock; whereupon, though my sedulous page would have had us to break our journey, and our fast, at the inn, I straightway set off for the academy, which was known to me, having daunted me when my grandmother showed it to me, and told me what it was, on an occasion when she took me with her on a journey to Bristol.

But that vexatious page was loitering again; and, wanting heart to be troubled with him, I took my portmanteau and dismissed him. Soon after, I saw him in a chat with some schoolboys. They stared at me as I passed on the other side of the way, and one of them (being a big, strong boy, having a round, rosy, smiling countenance) made some derisive comment upon me; whereupon the others laughed; which stung me to the quick. I went on, feeling the more wretched, knowing they were from the academy.

Being come before the walls, I stood awhile, looking upon the massy building, that rose gaunt and grey above the plantation, dark with ragged firs. Thereupon, with a sinking heart, I pushed open one of the gates and entered in.

It was the hour of sunset; and the topmost windows flashed in reflection. The rest were black with a swimming blackness that appeared to me in a phantasy to be thronged with eyes observing me, a small, contemptible, abject, forlorn creature, feebly carrying my burden. While I advanced up the avenue, I became sensible that my coat pocket bulged with a parcel of sweet cakes that my grandmother had set there, and the recollection of her in that place was a passionate misery to me; I had with desperate great gulps to swallow, hard put to it to contain my tears, that continually stood in my eyes.

At last, I stood at the door of that terrible mansion, pulled at the bell-chain, and stood waiting. I waited long; but my timorous summons was unanswered; and, while I doubted if I should ring again, the gates were thrown open with a loud sound, and I saw those three schoolboys I had met near the inn. They advanced briskly, talking and laughing; so that I wondered how in such a place they had the heart. But I feared them with a sort of shadowy dread; and, when, upon their approaching nearer, the big boy called to me, asking insolently who I was, I answered with a shaking voice.

"I am come," said I, "to be a scholar here."

They all laughed broad at this; and the big boy made sport of me.

"O ho!" cried he, "he is come to be a scholar here! A scholar, ho! ho! and we took him for a cry-baby!"

Hereupon he made a noise like weeping, and the rest shouted with jeering laughter; I knew that my page had betrayed me. My heart was ready to burst with the passion of misery that surged within me and overflowed with scalding tears; but, moving blind, my hand came against the bell-handle; and, laying hold on it, I pulled like mad: upon which those schoolboys immediately absconded themselves behind a laurel bush that stood beside the portal (for their proper entry was by the side-door). In the next moment, the door was opened by a tall footman, that stared at me while I seemed to myself to dwindle down to nothing in his sight.

"Well," cried he, and stopped. "Well, this beats cock-fighting, it do. Why, I took you for a markis, at least. What mean you by a-pulling of the bell fit to peal the house down?"

I answered, with a faint small voice, that I did it unwittingly, and was sorry for it; and he let me in, cursing and swearing to himself in a husky low voice, and, pushing me through the hall, thrust me into a handsome, large chamber.

"The master will come," said he, with a surly tone, and left me.

I stood looking before me in the dim light, yet scarce with observation, at a sculptured bust, set upon a pedestal, that represented a broad, good-humoured physiognomy, having curled hair and a beard, and a thick, turned up nose. But the sight of it startled my thoughts, at last, with the notion that it did represent Doctor Thompson himself (being the pedagogue's name); and whilst I attentively stared on it, taking a little comfort, the door was opened.

There entered an ancient, tall, ungainly man that stooped very much, who stepped to me with extraordinary jerky movements like a crab's. He had curled hair and a beard like the bust. But I knew not what to make of it, whether it could be the same; for his countenance was rather meagre, lugubrious, and severe than jocular, and his nose, though fleshy, not a jot like the bust.

This dismal grim visage quite dashed the comfort I had gotten from the object; and, whilst I stood staring on the person, he cried in a harsh, grating voice, "Well, sir? Well, sir? Well, sir? You have a tongue in your head, haven't you? You should have prepared yourself for me. You should have had your words ready. How, pray, have you employed your mind since your entry here?"

"Your portrait," said I, with halting words, lifting my hand up towards the bust.

But a great flush came over his face; and thereupon I discerned on a sudden, that his curled hair was nothing more than a wig.

"My portrait!" said he, grinning on me.

He began to step up and down, taking snuff from a big silver box, with a motion of tweaking his nose up, scattering much upon his clothes, that were very slovenly.

"Hm! my portrait!" said he, "You have good eyes in your head, boy. Is it like me, think you?"

"It's not much like you," said I; but his face twisted in so wry a look as made me repent that I ever did.

"Not?" cried he, with a lowering brow. "Not like me? But you did take it for me, didn't you?"

"Yes," said I. "I am very sorry. Perhaps it is like you."

"To be sure it is!" he cried vehemently. "You're no better than a fool, boy. How should you have taken it for me, else? Answer me that?"

But I could not; and, while I stood looking confused upon the floor, he, on a sudden, shoved a chair under the pedestal and sate down in it.

"Tut! tut! You shall see the likeness soon. Look upon this face and upon that," said he, tapping on his curled wig and pointing upwards. "So! You perceive it, don't you?"

"I do begin to perceive it," said I.

"To be sure you perceive it," said he. "It's patent to all. You're a great booby, and I've wasted a vast deal of time with you."

"I know who you are," he continued pompously, taking snuff and tweaking his nose up. "I have received letters from your grandmother.

You are come to be instructed here; and it's no small privilege, let me tell you, and no small honour neither, to be instructed in the academy of one, that, not only in physiognomy," said he, writhing his face and pointing to the bust, "but also in understanding, look you, bears so close a character to the philosopher, Socrates!"

He pronounced the name with slow and solemn emphasis, rolling his eyes and writhing his face after a doleful manner very hideous. Thereafter, he pulled the bell-rope; and, when the footman that had opened to me entered, he told him, with an horrible contortion, to take me to the schoolroom.

"Remove him immediately out of my sight!" said he sharply, stamping with his foot. "He is nothing but a fool."

"But tell me," said he, calling the man back, "who was that illustrious great sage that instructed, not corrupted (which was a most notorious error), the Athenian youth?"

"The philosopher, Socrates," said the footman, standing stiff beside the door, bawling out the words, as if he was announcing an arrival at some grand assembly.

"Notable also," answered the pedagogue, nodding his head, "was the poet, John Milton, who not only taught boys, but also writ his *Accedence Commenced Grammar*; and, reverting to the ancients, why need I mention the name of Cato, the Elder? Or, among the moderns, the erudite Erasmus?"

With these observations, he dismissed us.

I followed the tall footman through the hall, down some steps, and along an ill-lit passage, that did smell very musty; wherein a shrill sound of voices came muffled. Having opened a door at the end, he thrust me in, the voices coming in a great sound and then ceasing suddenly.

I felt at first as though I had entered some savage den; but became sensible it was a long, low room, lighted with two great lanterns that hung from the beam, and furnished with many desks and benches, in the spaces between which there stood a company of schoolboys: among whom I spied that big boy, having a babe-like countenance, that made such sport of me. He was the first to speak.

"Why," said he, jeering at me, "here comes the scholar!"

He was abridged by a burst of laughter that stunned my senses; and immediately they all came crowding about me, jeering, grimacing, and grinning at me. I stood in a sort of stupor; but my readers could never think what was in my thoughts; yet scarce in my thoughts neither, for 'twas but a peal of sounding words. 'Twas a tag from the Psalms, that I often read to my grandfather: *And many dogs are come about me*. So it run in my head; and, after a strange manner, it solaced me.

They continued to persecute me, asking many questions too ridiculous to be set down. But when, on my returning them no answer, they begun to hale me this way and that, to tweak my nose, pull my hair, and the like, my spirit awoke in a passion of grief and rage, and I struck blindly out at them with all my strength; nay, with more than my ordinary strength (I have said I was exceeding strong); for a frenzy came over me.

I was as one possessed. Instead of the pain, while they persecuted me, I was sensible of an exultation; and I flung out upon them, shouting the words of the psalm. They yielded in panic and confusion; but the big boy held still and his round, smiling, babe-like face appeared as in a crimson mist before my eyes. I struck at it in an extremity. My clenched fist beat hard and numb; the crimson mist turned to pitchy darkness, and I sunk upon the floor in a swound.

When I came to my senses, I lay in darkness. But my mind was heavy and numb; so that I could not think what was befallen me and was content to rest still. I slowly perceived I lay upon a bed, with my clothes on, and that my face was bruised and cut. In the same moment I heard a sound of boys conversing with low tones.

"Yes," said one. "He was dead for sure. I spied through the keyhole and saw him. He lay on the couch, and a sheet over him. It set me all on a tremor, and—"

He stopped; for the other abridged him.

"Nay," said he, "tell me tomorrow. But won't he be hanged? I mean the crazy fool that killed him."

"Yes, he will be hanged for sure. I heard the Doctor bid old Pompey bear a letter to the justice."

"Say you so? Why, then, we may expect a play-day tomorrow."

"Speak softer, you fool you! Yes, that's true. But I can't but admire the fellow. He was a brave fighter. How he did pitch into us! I tell you I have a great mind to warn him, so he could slip out and 'scape."

"O! I should not if I was you. They might hang you in his stead."

"You speak like an antic. And who would know, you fool you? I have a mind to it, I tell you!"

"'Tis you that speak like an antic. Don't you see it would come out if he was took?"

The other answered not, and both were silent, while I lay fearfully wondering if they could hear my heart knocking, it did sound so loud. Anon one of them spoke again.

"Fletcher," said he, "do you think he will be hanged?"

"I hope he will," said the other. "But let me sleep. I shall dream of the sport tomorrow."

"A wretch! a rascal! I'll fight you tomorrow, Fletcher! I'll near murder you. I'll pound your head. There's something to dream of for you."

He spoke almost loud; and the voice of another boy came drowsily, asking what the matter was. Whereupon, after a hurried whispering between them that sounded very fierce, they ceased; and no sound was heard save the breathings of the sleepers. But one of those twain kept turning upon his bed; and, when an hour was passed (an hour, and more, it seemed to me), he called softly to the other, asking if he waked. Having no answer, he called again, with the like issue; and soon after, he sat up (for I could descry him in his nightgown), got out of bed, and, having looked closely upon the other boy, stepped softly to my side.

"Do you hear me?" said he in my ear. "Can you rise up and walk? Speak soft."

"Yes," said I.

"Come, then," said he. "Do not speak. You must 'scape from here. Ask me no questions, but come. Step soft."

So I rose up, and followed him to the door; which he cautiously opened. After listening awhile, we went out and begun to descend the dark stairs. They creaked under our tread, and once very loud, so that we stood alarmed. Yet no answer came, and there was no sound save the clicking of the clock on the gallery. We came to the hall; thence down to the passage, where he opened a door and entered, and I after him.

"He hath his keys here," said he, searching with his hand along the wall. Having found the key that he wanted, being hung upon a pin, he returned into the passage and led me to the side-door, which he unlocked and opened.

I was full of gratitude to him, with the most affectionate solicitude lest his charitable services to me should bring him into trouble; but he would not suffer me to speak of it, bidding me quickly be gone.

So I parted from him stepping out into the dark night. Indeed, 'twas pitchy dark; but I groped my way from tree to tree down the avenue to the gates, and so departed that insufferable place.

I turned blindly along the road, going headlong on through the darkness, and, came, at length, by devious courses into the countryside. Thence I traversed a long lane, meeting with no living creature save a rat, that run scurrying into the ditch; and so forth upon meadows; whence, passing nigh a wood, on a sudden, a loud crying of owls near scared me out of my wits.

Now, the first hazard of my escape being past, I begun, at first dully, then with lively distress, to dwell upon my guilt (as I thought it); and I seemed to myself doubly a murderer, doubly damned; a soul infallibly lost, meet for the infernal fires; so that the torment of my thoughts increased and begun to be more than I could bear. I had read *Paradise Lost*, a copy of that grand poem being among my grandfather's books; and these lines started up in my recollection:

> *And that must end us, that must be our cure,*
> *To be no more; sad cure; for who would loose,*
> *Though full of pain, this intellectual being.*

"Who would loose?" cried I, passionately. "That would I! That would I!"

I endeavoured to have prayed, but I could not; and the torment swelled intolerable. There came, on a sudden, a sort of terrific flashing in my head as if I should go mad. And so verily, I believe, I should have done, if the powers of nature in me had not yielded, so that my senses were benumbed in a moment; and, sinking upon the grass, I fell into a sort of opiate sleep.

CHAPTER IV

His Acquaintance with Mr. Huxtable

'Twas broad day when I woke, the sun beating strong upon me. My mind laboured blind and tumultuous; my head ached with a dull throbbing, and my limbs were stiff and cramped. Yet a sense near joy came over me as I looked upon the country; where, over against me, a wood reared as a high, green island in a meadow-sea all blithe and gay with wild flowers. But soon I recollected how I came to be in that place.

I was hungry and thirsty; yet to have sought food and drink at a cottage, or farm, I durst not; and the issue of it was, I went and hid myself in the wood. And, lying in the thicket, my thoughts begun to settle in deep despair, or turned wildly to crazy inventions. Nay, I, who had always so great a dread of highwaymen, did think even to become one myself! I was, methought, predestinated to murder; and it seemed but a step from the unwitting to the intentional act. Though (said I) I was born to hang, I would live while I could, and, having waited until night came, waylay and murder some traveller, falling upon him with a bludgeon contrived in the wood. I was, no doubt, bemused in a sort of frenzy or delirium; for a sense of desperate hardihood possessed me, such as ordinarily, though never so driven, I could scarce have known.

From the madness of such an enterprise—at least, from the folly of such intentions—I was delivered by the coming, about sunset, of a pedestrian. This was a sailor, as appeared by his rolling gait (also he wore large ear-rings and a red cloth bound about his head), having a full, round countenance that looked rather pale and sallow than swarthy like the hue of a seafaring man.

No doubt, in a little altering my posture the better to have observed him, I made a rustling sound in the undergrowth; but, however, he must have possessed extraordinary sharp ears to have heard it, as he did, coming immediately to a stand and looking attentively towards the thicket where I lay. Thereupon, stepping to the place, he thrust into it with his stick, taking me in the ribs.

"Hey!" cried he, as I roared for pain. "What manner of rabbit, or weasel, have we here? Come out on't! Come out this minute, or I'll stir ye. They call me Obadiah; and I poke the fire. So."

He dug me shrewdly in the ribs again while he spoke; so that I came out roaring at his feet.

"I be Obadiah Moon; and I can sing a toon," said he, grinning at me while I writhed myself in the grass. "I be Obadiah Moon; and I sings little cherubs a sweet toon."

But, on a sudden, his face changed, his lips pursing craftily as he took thought. "There, never mind a jest, messmate!" said he, "I did but mean it merrily. There's younkers aboard ship makes a sport on me for my name, d'ye see? So that's how I sarves 'em, perdition take 'em!"

Hereupon such fury seized on him as distorted his face; and, with dreadful curses, he told me how he had murdered one of those ship-boys for so deriding him.

"I made no sport of your name," said I, trembling and shuddering at him.

"No," said he, "that's true. But 'tis like so, messmate, 'tis like so. I be gotten in the manner on't, d'ye see? I be gotten into an habitude. So, when I spies a younker such as you are (meaning no offence to ye), why, I goes for to lay un aboard without a hail. So you'll think no more on't—will ye? And, lookee, here's a silver shilling for your own."

Thereupon, after fumbling in his belt, he pulled out a shilling-piece and held it up in the rays of the sun; but when I would have taken it, he folded his fist upon it, saying:

"A silver shilling for your own, for a-bearing of a letter; but, no, look'e here, here's a cur'osity for ye. I know boys likes cur'osities; though you're more of a grown man than a boy, as I can see."

With this, he returned the shilling to his belt, and pulled out from the pocket of his coat a rich and curious sea-shell, brown and white, and showed it to me in his hand.

"There be an handsome pretty thing," said he "come all the way from China. And heark'ee," said he, and set it to my ear. "Heark'ee to the voice of the sea. Bear it about with you, and it will sing to you howsoever far inland you be."

"Where would you have me bear your letter to?" asked I, looking at the sea-shell.

"Not above a pace or two, messmate," said he. "Two or three meadows hence. Over yonder there, hard by the mill on your larboard bow. *Mr. John Huxtable, Ridley Farm, near to Bristol in the county of Somerset*," said he, mouthing the words. "And thank'ee kindly; but mind ye, I trust ye, and, trusting ye, I won't go for to say what'll happen to ye if you don't deliver this-here letter. And you'll deliver it into his hand. Mind that!"

"Give it to me," said I; "and I will bear your letter for you."

"Nay," said he, grinning broad and returning it to his pocket. "This is a *transaction*, as the scriveners say; and ships don't carry their rudders afore, but at the stern. Likewise with apes—you knows where their tails be. I'll not give it to you before you delivers my letter; but when you delivers my letter, then I'll give it to you."

He put the letter into my hand, glaring at me suddenly with an evil eye. Thereupon, with a grin and a smirk and a "Thank'e, messmate. Thank'e kindly," he was gone, betaking himself round the shoulder of the wood.

I made my way across a meadow to the farm, being a great pile, having many roofs, that stood over against a windmill. I could see no appearance of life in the place, neither of man nor beast; and the sails of the windmill stood still. But scarce was I come in sight of the house, beyond the meadow, but cheerful thoughts begun to possess my mind. The sun was just set, and a comfortable light tinged the landscape and shone ruddy and gold upon the walls and roofs. A sense of home and haven solaced me while I entered by the wicket-gate and stepped up the path to the porch. So I rapped at the door.

'Twas opened by a big man, who wore his beard like a sailor, almost down to his waist. Upon my telling him that I bore a letter to *Mr. John Huxtable*, he took it in his hand, and bad me, with a deep tone, to follow him into a room; where he set light to two candles.

"Sit you down while I read over this letter," said he, breaking the seal.

What with his prodigious beard and moustaches, his eyebrows as great tufts, and his great hook nose, he had a fierce and even forbidding character; but this (as I now understand the matter) was through stress and effort and bitter brooding. Young and unpractised in observation and understanding though I was, I yet vaguely perceived in his face and wide furrowed brow, the mark and signature of some corroding sorrow.

The chamber was of a good size, and was but sparely furnished with a plain ordinary table and four chairs; but there stood an elegant carved desk beside the wall, bearing, upon tall silver sconces, the candles, that cast a dim illumination.

The man went and sat him down there to read his letter, spreading forth his elbows upon the desk; a great big fellow, with his huge shoulders and large towelled head like a lion's.

There were two pictures hung up by the wall over against him, being, one of them, the portraiture of a most beautiful lady, whose countenance, with its bright blue eyes and her golden hair, seemed irradiated with a kind of starry grace. The other represented a little child, having fair cheeks, bright blue eyes, and golden hair like the lady's, but that it was lighter, which hung waving about his shoulders.

Now, while I looked upon them, the tall candles in their sconces and those delectable pictures, made me think of the church which that ancient Spanish woman took me into when I was a child, and of the priests in their gaudy vestments, kneeling before the altar; for it seemed to me that the man who sat huddled forward upon the desk, made in his spirit a sore petition.

I observed that the letter I had conveyed to him was but brief, being writ only on the one side; but he did read it over and over, and then appeared to fall into a muse. At last, he turned about in his chair, and sat gazing upon me, but so as if he did not see me and looked through me. It did make me feel insubstantial like a phantom; and glad I was, when, after fetching a deep sigh, he spoke, stroking of his beard.

"You don't look like a pirate's boy," said he.

"A pirate's boy," said I in perplexity. "Was that sailor that gave me the letter a pirate?"

"So the letter was given you by a sailor," said he. "But how came you to fall in with this sailor?"

So I related my adventure beside the wood, rehearsing all that the man had said to me. He attentively hearkened, and then began to question me about myself, the wise, understanding, charitable look in his eyes prompting me to begin my story without fear; and, indeed, it was a great comfort to tell it out. I had no more diffidence presently than if I spoke to my poor grandmother, and much more consolation.

"Well," said he when I had ended, "I think it was a good wind that brought you here; and, if you have a mind to it, you shall stay with me. But will you do me a piece of service, I wonder? The sailor who gave you the letter will wait in a court in the town tomorrow night for an answer. It's a matter of great concernment to me; but I may not go myself; neither may I send anyone else but you, being the bearer of the letter. You have taken—haven't you?—a fear of that sailor; and I dare say he is a great rogue. But I don't believe you will be endangered, or I wouldn't ask you to go."

I told him I was very willing to bear his letter, feeling, indeed, that I would do anything I could for him; and he thanked me, looking kindly and affectionately on me.

"But what if I be seen and taken?" said I; "for I fear they will watch for me in the Bristol streets."

"There's a hazard of it," said he; "but, if you are taken. I shall deliver you, have no fear."

And, indeed, my fear left me while he spoke; and, although my readers think them but big words, yet I make no more question now, being come into years, than I did then when I was but a boy, that, if I had been taken by the watch, he would have delivered me.

He rose up now, and lit a lantern; and thereupon, saying that I must be sharp set after my long fasting, he went to the larder to provide my supper; which I ate heartily enough, as you may suppose; while, having sat down at his desk, he wrote some letters, the wrinkles in his forehead appearing very plain in the candlelight.

He asked me afterward did I know the Temple Church? I told him, yes. "Well, then," said he, "there's a little back-street, called *Baker's Court*, between the churchyard and the *Shakespeare* tavern, nigh to the fountain that has an effigy of Neptune. There will the sailor be come tomorrow, about two hours after sunset, for my answer. Do you set out at seven by the clock on the chimney-piece. I must rise betimes and be away all day, for I have much to do; but I shall be returned, I hope, before you are."

"Here is my answer," said he, rising up and taking one of the letters he had written into his hand. "It's a matter of serious moment, and must not miscarry. See, I have writ the hour for your setting out on this paper, as well as the style of the court; and I set it (said he, stepping to the chimney) beside the clock, with the letter also. Do you know the way from here?"

I asked him was the farm near *Redcliffe Street*. "Yes," said he, "if you look out at the window of your bedchamber in the morning, you will see it before you across the meadows." "I know the way, then," said I, "very well: through *Redcliffe Street* to St. *Thomas' Street*, and thence through *Mitchell Lane* into *Temple Street*."

He nodded his head, "Mind you do not slip the hour," said he; "but I am sure that I can trust you. And now, as you must be tired after such a rough day, I will light you to bed. Come, you shall lie in my bedchamber; I shall soon contrive a couch for you."

While he spoke, taking one of the candlesticks, he stepped to the other door (for there were two), and led the way up a steep stair. Thence we entered a chamber that was plain and neat. The bed was but small, being rather a pallet or truckle bed.

"We shall not need much bed-clothes on such a summer's night," said he, "and can make a shift between us."

Thereupon, he pulled the mattress from his bed, bed-clothes and all; and, having disposed it orderly upon the floor, he made his own bed of the bare sacking and some of the bed-clothes. So he left me to my repose.

I lay contemplating the strange, surprising turn my fortune had taken; while the silence of the night was sometimes interrupted by the monotonous loud chirping of moorhens. When, at last, I slept, it was to dream of extraordinary occurrences on the sea.

CHAPTER V

Strange Mysterious Adventures Before Embarking

When I awoke in the morning, I saw my breakfast was set on a table by my bedside. On my plate there was a note of writing, which was to tell me I should find some books in a chest that was in my bedchamber, to pass the time.

From this it was plain he desired me to stay indoors until I went to deliver his letter; and so I did, reading in Captain Dampier's *Voyages* (that I did often delight to read in after), which moved me to dreams of strange adventures, that (as I imagined) Mr. Huxtable would bring to pass; although, in an exploration I afterward made of the house, the void chambers and passages and the view of the deserted farm, did somewhat dash my expectations; nor could I but wonder that Mr. Huxtable, who did not seem to be an ordinary farmer, should dwell thus in this bare farmhouse, what manner of man he was, and what his business with the vagabond sailor could be.

At the appointed hour, I set forth with the letter, which was inscribed to *Mr. Obadiah Moon*. The evening was fair; but dusk was fallen when I arrived the court.

The sailor was not yet come, and I took up my station in a corner. It was a small mean place, lying between the back of the old tavern and the churchyard, in the Ropemakers' quarter, and looked even meaner under the yellow moon. There stood another ancient tavern, called *The Crab's Well*, over against the *Shakespeare*; and, being both of them infested already with the evening drinkers, they gave forth continually a roaring sound.

Now, although this kind of adventure is well enough to read of in a story, it is very little agreeable in the actual experience; as I have heard soldiers say, complaining of the privations and miseries of the wars; and either our romantic authors know little, or nothing at all, of the adventures and exploits that they relate, or, if they do, they know by art to extract the fangs of horror. A sense of foreboding began to oppress my thoughts. I eagerly expected the sailor's coming, that I might be done with the business, and yet I feared him, too; not, indeed, lest he should offer me any actual violence, but of something shadowy and undefined; and, if I had not taken so strong an assurance of Mr. Huxtable (and I never once conceived any doubt or mistrust concerning him), my dismal thoughts might have tempted me to make off; but then, where could I have gone? for sure I could never have taken the face to return, with my errand unaccomplished, to the farm.

While I thus stood oppressed with these dismal thoughts, sometimes a roisterer, issuing from the tavern, passed by to enter the churchyard. Once an ancient woman passed, stooping and walking with a staff, the moonlight shining upon her face, that was consumed with some dreadful disease; which nigh turned me sick for horror. Soon after I saw the sailor enter the court. I immediately stepped to him with Mr. Huxtable's letter in my hand.

"What cheer, messmate?" cried he after a jovial manner while he took the letter. "Hove to, was you? Well, thank'e for standing by."

I immediately made off; but he called to me, bidding me stand and stay. He spoke in a kind of horrid snarling voice; so that I dashed forward wildly, scarce escaping him as he made a pass upon me with his stick.

Thereupon, he began to chase me with furious and dreadful, savage threatenings; but I only run the faster, and left him quite behind. At length, looking fearfully back while I took breath, I observed he had yielded the pursuit, and was fallen into his ordinary pace. But he raised a shout at me which put me to my heels again, and I was soon come to the skirts of the town, and presently in view of the farmhouse; a light in the window making a comfortable signal across the dark meadow.

Mr. Huxtable opened to me even while I knocked; and, when I had contented him by telling him I had delivered his letter, he took me into the room, where my supper was set.

"But you need not have made such haste," said he; for I still breathed short with running. "Did the man say anything to you?"

And when I told him, "I am heartily sorry for it," said he. "I can't understand why he should chase you. But it is no matter. Sit you down and eat. But what was his intent, I wonder."

He began to pace up and down, with his brows bended together, sometimes plucking at his beard. I wondered, while I ate, if he would tell me anything of the matter; and, as though he perceived my thoughts, he said presently:

"You shall hear my story, lad; but not now. Let it suffice that I am about to embark in an adventure over the sea, and my ship lies in the river. I go to seek my son, my little son. Look! there be his picture hung up upon the wall, over against his mother's!"

His voice quavered while he spoke, and dwindled to a desolate sound. A weight of sadness came over me, and the tears started in my eyes; which perceiving, he looked affectionately on me, saying:

"But I shall find my son. You two are of an age. If God send that he be restored to me, you shall be as brothers."

I suppose, I was still distraught with my miserable adventures; for I begun to weep outright. He started up upon this, and, setting his hand upon my head and stroking my hair. "Nay, nay, lad!" said he. "You must not weep. But, indeed, you are like my son. Come! you shall go with me. I'll take you to sea with me in my ship."

This stopped my tears effectually; and I told him how glad I was for it, and asked him eagerly when it would be. He told me in a few days; and thereupon, after I had helped him to remove the supper things, and he had set the candles on the table, he began to entertain me with his travels to foreign parts, describing strange, outlandish places that he had seen, and far peoples, their manners and customs, and the like, which increased my delectable expectations.

Yet there came in the midst, as a sad shadow, the thought of my grandmother, that in my late alarms and distresses I had scarce once remembered. My heart sunk and my mind was overcast in a moment. But he, perceiving my dejection and enquiring the occasion of it, when I had told him, said that I should write a letter to my grandmother, acquainting her with what had passed at the Academy, how I had escaped and fallen in with a good Samaritan, and that, though the time might needs be something protracted, I would certainly go to her as soon as I possibly could.

In these terms, indeed, I did write to her; and it comforted me.

In the next three days, Mr. Huxtable was away upon the business of his ship. I stayed close indoors, diverting myself by reading, especially *Don Quixote*, which was among those books in the chest.

But I was formed to distil the sadness of things; at least, so conditioned by the character of my childhood. I did weep beside the death-bed of the *Pathetic Knight* as passionately as any that in the story knelt there, and saw the laughter of the foregoing acts through a misty glass. It is a faithful parable; for every man, worthy of the name, is a *Don Quixote*, or a *Sancho Panza* (the rest are dull scoffing fools); he is wrought true by his delusions; his heroic antics and blunders move no mocking laughter.

Sometimes I went to look out at the window. But the prospect of the bare countryside, extended large in the bright sun, and the deserted farmyard and windmill, afflicted me with loneliness, and I soon returned to my book. Indeed, on the last occasion (being on the third day), I suffered something worse; for, as it seemed to me, while I looked forth upon the mill, a dark terrible face did gaze on me at the upper window.

The appearance passed shadowy; and, setting it down to phantasy, I did not tell Mr. Huxtable when he returned after noon, lest he should think me timorous.

Soon after sunset, he took me with him to the riverside, which lay about two miles distant, to help him convey some things aboard the ship; I bearing some baggage, he carrying those portraits of his wife and child.

The ship, that lay hauled close beside the bank, was but ordinary in size, being 200 tons burden, somewhat old-fashioned, with her high, sloping poop. But much of the upper part had been cut down, especially all the heavy carved work belonging to the stern, which made her, in some sort, of a maimed appearance. I was much taken with the figurehead, all glistening white, in the form of a woman extended above the waters, her neck and head outstretched, and her great protuberant eyes fast closed, as if she prayed, with her clasped hands, and sped ever onward.

I became sensible that Mr. Huxtable also stood gazing on it.

"Look, 'tis a type of our state and condition in this world," said he solemnly. "The ship is the toiling manful part; the woman, retired in stillness and contemplation, is the speeding soul."

We went on board as he spoke, and betook ourselves to the forecastle; wherein, after entering, we beheld, in the lamplight, two seaman reclined upon the floor on either side, with their heads resting against the lockers.

"Is this how they keep their watch?" said Mr. Huxtable. "What do they mean?" cried he, laying hold upon one of them by the shoulder. "He is drunk," said he, giving him a shake; for the man did not come to his senses, though he did shake him sufficiently, but only murmured in his beard.

"Well, this is strange," said Mr. Huxtable; "for it seems they've drunk but little, if this is all they had."

While he spoke, he pointed with his finger to a bottle that stood on a locker beside a cup. "Rum," said he, taking and smelling of it. It was three parts full.

Hereupon, he went to work with the other fellow, who proved not so deep; for his eyes opened soon after, and he woke up, though very lumpish and stupid.

"How come you to be in this drunken drench?" asked Mr. Huxtable sternly, when the man was sufficiently in his wits to understand him. "Is this how you keep your watch, sirrah?"

"I be not drunk," answered the sailor, who was a great burly fellow, and repeated, "I be not drunk," while he staggered to his feet; but immediately after sunk back upon the locker. "I knows not what we ail," said he, glancing his eyes aside at his fellow, who now shifted his posture and begun to breathe very hard. "We did drink no more'n a noggin between us, with water in it. It was never so afore; for every evening we took a dram, your honour, what time we was changing watch. I swear to ye, 'twas no more, and, by token, you can see the bottle. Look, 'tis nigh full!"

"That's true," said Mr. Huxtable, looking hard at him. "Where did you get this bottle of rum?"

"I had it of a hawker, your honour," said he, "as come and hailed the ship yesterday soon after dark fell. Sure there must be something amiss with it, which has put us in a distemper, though it tasted good."

"A *hawker*?" said Mr. Huxtable, handing his beard. "What was his appearance? Can you describe him particularly?"

"Nay," said the man, "he seemed but a common or ordinary hawker, but I never thought to take any particular notice of him. He was summat of a tall man, and spoke thick in his beard, muttering hoarse, which is all as I can mind me of."

"Well," said Mr. Huxtable, after taking a pace up the forecastle, "it looks as though the rum had been meddled with, and it's possible an attempt will be made to rob the ship. This puts me in a quandary; for I must return to the farm tonight—nay, as soon as I can, yet I am not willing to leave you by yourselves. Your mate seems to breathe easier. Let us see if we can awaken him. Go, fetch me some water to lave his face."

Upon this, the big seaman rose up from the floor, and went, with unsteady steps, to the further end of the forecastle, whence he returned with a bowl full.

"Begging your pardon, your honour," said he, "I knows on a powerful remedy in such a case as this is. I had it from one of the old privateers. Give me leave."

Hereupon, he went down on his knees, raised the bowl to his lips, and made as if he would drink it down. Then, with his mouth full, he turned himself to his mate, and begun to blow it out in a thin small spray in his eyes and ears. After he had done this a second time, the sleeper presently sighed and opened his eyes, and in no long time was as much recovered as the other.

Mr. Huxtable, nevertheless, seemed still in doubt what he should do.

"It were all one," said he, "if they had found you sleeping. I mean, if this hawker should be one of some thieving gang. They would get but little on the ship, and less that I should lack. Not that I think there's any likelihood of an attempt; but it looks strangely. Let us get out in the fresh air."

He stepped to the door while he spoke; but observing that the night was become pitch dark, he returned, desiring one of those seamen to provide him with a lamp from a cabin in the tween-decks, against our return to the farmhouse. So the man went and brought one, and kindled it; and Mr. Huxtable bade me take it and lead the way, which I accordingly did; but, coming out on the deck, I stood stock still, glaring; for, chancing to look towards the river bank, that dreadful apparition I saw, or thought I saw, at the window of the mill, was looking upon me above the gunnel. 'Twas but for a moment in a glancing flare; for I let go of the lantern, that fell cluttering upon the deck, and the light went out.

"The face!" cried I, clutching hold on Mr. Huxtable by the arm, "the dreadful face. I saw it at the mill and in the wood. 'Twas there yonder above the bulwarks."

"Why, what do you mean?" said he, stepping up and down in the darkness. "There's no one at the mill. 'Tis shut up. This is your phantasy—but hark!" cried he, standing still; for a harsh savage cry was heard—whether of man or beast was obscure, and there came a small sound as of running. It was on the river-bank, towards the town.

"Come on, my lads!" said Mr. Huxtable; and, not staying to kindle the lantern, he mounted to the gunnel and leapt over upon the bank, being followed by the seamen and by me.

"Scatter, and make a wider sweep," said he, while we ran, "but not so as to be beyond call. 'Tis clear open country this way, so you need not fear to run upon an obstacle."

But, though it was as he said, and our eyes, also, were become accustomed to the darkness, 'twas no pleasant manner of running; and glad was I when, after cruising along some distance without seeing or hearing anything of our quarry, he yielded the attempt, and we returned to the ship.

He told us that he would now return with me to the farm, and bad the two seamen to betake themselves thither betimes in the morn, to help him convey some things aboard the ship.

"You may rest easy in the ship," added he. "Very like 'twas a false alarum; but if there was anybody, he will attempt nothing further after the scare we have given him. But sink the bottle of rum in the river."

"Ay, your honour, that I will," said the big sailor. "May perdition take it!"

He stepped on board the ship while he spoke; and the other followed. Soon he appeared at the side with the bottle in his hand.

"If there be a woman goddess to this-here river," said he, "as I have heard tell there be in some rivers, here be summat for her to drink me a health," and cast the bottle overboard. The other seaman kindled the lamp, which was not broken by the fall, and brought it to Mr. Huxtable. A few moments after, I heard another sound in the river close under the ship. I told Mr. Huxtable, but he said it would be but a whirl in the tide, or, mayhap, a water rat.

"And what else do you think it should be?" asked he. "Do you suppose it is the robber absconding himself in the river?" said he, laughing at me.

But, however, he took a turn along by the river side, lowering his lamp so as to shine upon the sluggard black pool.

"Let us begone," said he, with a weary voice, turning his eyes away from the melancholy waters; and, nothing loth (for I begun to shiver acold), I started off beside him.

The night was chill, with a shrewd, rising, east wind; and, being both weary and hungry, I was glad when we arrived the farmhouse; where we made all snug and broiled some beef.

By the time we had finished supper, the wind was increased to a gale that roared wild about the house, shaking the doors and windows, or shifted about, moaning in the chimney. When we had removed our chairs beside the hearth, I asked Mr. Huxtable if he would tell me a traveller's tale. But "Nay," said he, "hearken rather to the tale of the wind! Hearken now!"

He leant forward, gazing on the pale glowing embers; and I heard it lonesome and remote and very solemn, whiffling in the chimney, crooning and circling in a rustling dance, dying insensibly away, and coming again, with a ghostly sound.

"It's like the still small voice in the Bible," said I; and he nodded gravely.

"And hark!" said he, as it rose with a furious blustering sound, "there comes the whirlwind."

He fell silent after that, seeming to brood in his mind, with a heavy brow and his eyes fixed sad and dreamy upon the glowing coals; and soon, becoming drowsy, I left him to take up my repose.

The wind now blew more steady, yet with no less force. The night was clear and shiny with stars; and, coming into my bedchamber, I saw the sails of the windmill whirling round. This scared me, I know not how, and put me in haste to get me between the bed-clothes, as if, forsooth, they were a protection against any terror in the world.

But I slept presently, and was translated to a region of brightness and efficacy inexpressible; from which enchanting dream I awoke in a wavering light that appeared brighter than day. 'Twas the glare of some conflagration near the house; and Mr. Huxtable stood at the lattice looking out.

I got quickly out of bed; and saw that it was the mill; for at the small lower window, a great flame streamed, waving and curling in the night; and thick smoke issued from the higher window mingled with sparks, that were instantly dispersed by the wind. The sails turned with a great clacker. But as I looked, I saw, to my astonishment, the sailor, Moon, and another with him, being a tall man, running along beside the further end of the wall. I did see them but for an instant; and, as it seemed to me, there was yet another with them, but being ahead, he whipped out of sight too soon to be descried.

"Why, what does he there?" cried I. "Did you mark him, that sailor? And who was he that was with him? and was there a third?" And I remembered, while I spoke, that dark terrible countenance I saw, looking forth upon me from the window of the mill, and afterwards on the quay when we went on board the ship.

"Ay," said Mr. Huxtable, staring out at the lattice, "'twas the sailor. But how he came to be there I can't fathom, or what the others could be. One of them did look strange. I shall examine into it when I see Moon on the ship, for he goes with us. But quick, put your clothes on! This blaze will rouse the town, and we must be gone. It is well that those seamen are come. I have let them in, and they wait below."

While I dressed, he went and fetched those two seamen whom we left on the ship; and we helped them convey two large chests, that stood in his bedchamber, down the stairs, and out to the porch; where they lifted them on a hand-barrow. In the meantime, the mill began to blaze with a great roaring sound, flames and smoke issuing as well from the windows as the door, and the turning sails, having kindled, whirled sparks and rags of fire down the wind.

It was near dawn when we departed the farmhouse (the two seamen trundling the barrow on before); so that attracted by the conflagration, we might soon expect some early-risers; for it illumined the night as a tempest of flame, casting great fires; the wind seemed a-blaze!

But, however, we met with no man; neither, indeed, with any adventure, until, in passing through a wood about half way on our journey, I felt on a sudden that someone, or something observed me from underneath a bush. 'Twas dark, but not pitch dark; for there was a ruddy glow cast by the conflagration; and, turning quickly, I dimly discerned a face, dusky and grim, having prodigious glistening black eyes, and its brow running up monstrous narrow and high.

It vanished away even as I did see it; but I stood staring on the place, plucking Mr. Huxtable by the arm.

"Ah," cried I, "'twas a fiend! a frightful fiend! Did you not see it?"

"Nay, I saw nothing," said he, staring into the bush. "What was the appearance of it?"

So I described it to him, but he said it was but my phantasy. "We will not be hindered with it," said he. "You are overwrought and want sleep. Come, let us get aboard!"

But I was tormented, on a sudden, with this dreadful apprehension—that that face I beheld was the face of my grandfather haunting me in an infernal image; so that I went with a distracted and fearful mind. Mr. Huxtable, to have diverted me (as I suppose), began to tell me of the process of providing the ship, and that the Captain and our men would come aboard in the morning.

At length, taking me briskly by the arm (for he perceived that I lent but a dull ear, scarce indeed apprehending the sense): "Why what ails you, Will," said he, "to be so mopish and melancholy? You do not repent, do you, that you're going to sea?"

I told him, no, and begun, with halting words, to divulge that notion of my grandfather haunting me; from which horrible chimera he presently delivered me.

"As a lad," said he, "I also did suffer such tormenting whimsies; though of a different kind, and 'tis a common distemper of young and sensible minds. Nay, I was so troubled and plagued with 'em at last, I was like to have gone crazy; but I learnt a short way to be rid of them; which was nothing else but to thrust them forth immediately at their coming from my thoughts, and to shut and bar the door upon them, and keep it barred. They soon lost their hold, warping and warping when they could not get in, dwindling and fading into the moon-stuff that they were!"

"Not," added he, "that I deny supernatural visitations (which is the present trouble of your thoughts), since our life is environed round with mystery, and is itself the greatest mystery. We to ourselves are phantoms, in one way, and terrible phantoms too. But that to which we are phantoms (if you understand me) is the true and immortal part in us, which, being of God, ought not, and cannot be afeared of anything in this life, nor yet in the life to come."

This encouraged me to tell him of those dreadful imaginations of hell which my grandfather implanted in my mind, and the fear I had that I should be condemned to eternal fire for having occasioned his death and the schoolboy's also.

"I do not doubt," said he when I had ended, "that every one must needs pay the reckoning for his sins, and we have plenty of examples even in this life. *The Gods are just,* as Shakespeare says, *and of our pleasant vices make instruments to plague us;* but eternal fire is nothing but a figure admonishing us how dreadful evil is. As for those deaths of your grandfather and the schoolboy, I rather think they ran into it themselves. Your grandfather was a wretched creature; but the schoolboy's death is sad and grievous; but I do not think you are obliged to think on it further but as a memento to rule your passions. "But see!" (cried he, pointing with his finger) "there lies the ship. We shall be aboard presently, and then off to sea, which will soon clear all ghostly cobwebs from your mind."

I looked and saw the tall masts of the ship in the grey light as day began to peep above the river.

PART II

CHAPTER VI

The Voyage Commenced

As we arrived the bank of the river, we saw the lantern hauled down in the stern, and immediately after there was a whistle blown, shrill and long drawn out, striking sharp and cold as the dawn air. Mr. Huxtable told me it was the boatswain rousing up our men; and I saw him, in his blue boat-cloak, standing under the break of the poop.

We went on board, and Mr. Huxtable led the way aft to the cabin door; and, entering into the alley-way, we went to the cabin, where the lantern was lit, casting a bright shine upon the massy oak table. Thereupon, Mr. Huxtable, bidding me stay for him, stepped into his cabin, that stood on the starboard side, bearing the parcels that we had brought. But I being exceeding tired, went and reposed myself along the locker (having cushions on it) under the stern-window, and almost immediately sunk into a deep sleep.

When I awoke, the day was come, the sun shining bright through the cabin windows, that stood open. I saw Mr. Huxtable in discourse with two others at breakfast. One (being the Captain) was a brisk fleshy affable man, of a shaven, ruddy, cheerful countenance, very neatly dressed and wearing a powdered peruke. The other was of aspect more remarkable and strange, being tall and spare, having a long pale visage, the colour of a tallow candle, and lank dark hair. He was dressed in a black coat buttoned up to the neck. His look was gaunt, lantern-like, and vaguely lugubrious, affecting me with a sense of something dismal and shadowy in him, and his eyes kept restlessly turning, slanting with a black gleam. I endeavoured to have diverted my thoughts from this disquieting phantasy by attending to the discourse.

This was on a nautical topic, the Captain speaking much, after a smooth affected manner, choosing and tasting and mincing his words; the gaunt man holding silent, save when he was addressed; and then he answered in brief, muttering low and obscure, while his eyes kept turning from the Captain to Mr. Huxtable and back, like a slid panel. They shifted upon me suddenly as I lay observing him, which gave me a start; for 'twas as if they cast a hard glitter like metal. I stirred upon the locker; and Mr. Huxtable, perceiving that I was awake, called me to the table, making a place for me by his side; and Captain Blythe (as his name was), rising from his chair, made me a low bow, which not a little abashed me.

"I am your humble servant," said he, coming and shaking me by the hand after an affected manner. "'Tis not the first time I have entertained a young gentleman aboard my ship. Mr. Richard Roach (who, you know, is a kinsman to my Lord Heddlestone) some years past entrusted his son in my charge, being of such an age as you are, when he would have had him to see the world in a voyage to Italy. *Dick*, says he, to the young nobleman, *I charge you to honour and obey the Captain like a second father—an alter pater, as the Latin has it—which is more than he does to me* (said he in my ear), *the graceless young scamp!* 'Twas a brave young man, and of a noble bearing; an hopeful stem of such an illustrious stock. You know, don't you, that my Lord Heddlestone's family is one of the ancientest trees in the English peerage?"

I answered as properly as I was able, being quite overcome by this speech, of which the manner was not less preposterous than the matter (although I thought it very grand); while the eyes of the gaunt man, turning this way and that, made a shine, as it were a cross-flashing maze, in my imagination. Him the Captain now presented to me, being Mr. Falconer, the mate; who rose slowly from his chair and made me a bow, moving after a slow torpid manner and looking vacant on me. Mighty glad was I when they returned to their discourse; which gave me the more countenance to eat my breakfast.

Soon after, the Captain said that the tide of flood must now be spent, and 'twas time to weigh; whereupon, they all rose up to go to the deck; whither I followed them.

The ship was already swung out from the quay across the stream; and the Captain, standing beside the poop-rail, ordered to heave up the anchor.

Thereupon, the boatswain blew his whistle, and the men came running about the capstan, which, the bars being set, they began to turn, tugging round on tiptoe, with a hearty loud song; while the tight cable came straining in. Others swarmed the rigging to loose the topsails; as Mr. Falconer, standing on the forecastle, gave them charge.

Having a fine land breeze, our ship began to sail down the river, gathering way as they hoisted up the mizzen sail, and so onwards into the Channel. As we came round the bend over against Portishead, I looked out for my grandmother's house (for we sailed very near the shore) and saw the roof and upper windows. One of them was the window of her bedchamber, and I strained my eyes to observe it, wondering if she was yet risen and whether she might chance to look out and spy our ship, although I knew she could not have seen me or have any notion that I was on board. But my sight grew hazy with tears.

At last, we stood out to sea, gently rolling in the waves, with a cheerful noise of hauling and singing as our men hoisted up more and more sails.

It is a pleasure, says Sir Francis Bacon, *to stand upon the shore and to see ships tossed upon the sea*; and I, who had stood upon the shore when my grandmother took me, on an occasion, to Ilfracombe, watching a ship spreading her wings like a great fowl upon the water, did now, being on float, observe it with such delight as a young man knows, stepping forth in his imagination into the world, making toys of circumstance and substantial things; as, when he was a child, the other way, he seriously changed his playthings, with a child's enchantment, into their objects. And all the circumstance of this world is (to speak wisely) but matter for toys; all things are merely playthings, whether of a captain that hath a pride and pleasure in his ship, or of a boy, or a man that (like Mr. Falconer, as I shall relate) delighteth to fashion out little ships. The one sort discovers the child in the man, the other the man in the child.

This new and enchanting experience of being on a ship at sea, accordingly, did quite possess me, and chased away my sorrowful thoughts; but, if I had wanted any diversion, the choleric behaviour of the Captain (much belying his affable demeanour in the cabin) had well provided me.

This first appeared on the fifth day of our voyage, when we found we lay much nearer the Spanish coast than we had expected; which put the Captain in a choler. That another craft was in the same error, and the like predicament, did not appease but rather inflamed his anger; and he prowled from one side of our deck to the other like a caged beast, venting many very furious expressions. And upon other occasions, to see him strike his hands together, stamp his foot, dash his hat down, and run raging mad upon the least provocation, you would have supposed his antics had made him a laughing-stock, especially in his leaping back and forth, being such a short stout figure of a man, he appeared so ridiculous.

Our men, nevertheless, and notwithstanding *his bark was worse than his bite* (as the saying is), were much afraid of the Captain—all save one of them that cared nothing for his anger; and him, indeed, the Captain did always avoid, even in his extreme rages, and affronted but once in my knowledge, and then rather blundering blind at him than on purpose. This man seemed verily to cast over him a soothing spell; especially on one occasion when he was very angry with the carpenter (whose tardy manner of going to work was a continual offence to him); for, on his but catching his eye as he stood with his spyglass lifted up in a transport, I beheld the Captain to stand and falter, his arm sinking as if it was nerveless by his side, and he turned away murmuring.

He that had such power over the Captain was an old, hale, gentle, greybeard sailor—Giles Kedgley, by name—that not much consorted with the rest (though well liked by them all) and used a quaint fashion of discourse—I mean, in an ordinary seaman, although natural, as proceeding from something noble in him, and not strained, nor foppishly affected; for, no matter who he spoke with, whether Mr. Huxtable or the Captain, or plain Tom Nodkins, the carpenter's mate, 'twas ever with the same courtly and respectful style and manner of address.

But, commonly (as I say), he held himself apart; and, retired in his pious devotions, passed the most of his leisure time reading the Bible. In fair weather (his watch being done, or not yet begun) 'twas usual to see him squatted down in an angle of the bows, with his book laid open on his lap, his studious head inclined, quietly and solemnly droning to himself as his forefinger moved slowly across the page.

This was a reader of the Bible very different, indeed, from my terrible grandfather. He is pleasant and gracious in my recollection as I see him in his lofty nook (being quite sequestered within himself as in a quiet cell), sometimes looking up from his Bible with his eyes kindled, having a soft still radiance in them as of the shining of an intelligible flame.

To Mr. Huxtable the Captain was commonly civil and respectful; and he treated me tolerable well, though not so affable as in my first meeting with him which was scarce to be expected. To Mr. Falconer, however, unless in the way of command and process of ordering the ship, he did speak but seldom, even at meals, and on deck was wont to use him almost worse than the common seamen. 'Twas a wonder how Mr. Falconer could bear with it. Yet he did suffer it as patiently, or rather carelessly and coldly (for it seemed not to touch him) as his own conduct of the men was frigid and aloof.

As for them, 'twas plain they misliked him. They sullenly stood off from him, and did his bidding only under constraint. Sometimes, if neither the Captain nor Mr. Huxtable was on deck, they murmured openly at him; especially the boatswain (being a lean, morose, active man); but he never took any notice of such insubordination, and I do believe, if they had derided him to his face, it would not have moved him any the more. If water, and not blood, had run in his veins, he could not have appeared more wanting in spirit; so much the less wonder that he provoked the Captain's spleen, as he did, even as the inflammatory sprinkling of water on a smithy forge.

In two only particulars gave he any signs of animation; and in them indeed, he was perfectly engaged. One was but a boy's diversion, being the making and rigging of little ships, but having such strange outlandish figureheads as (I know not how otherwise to express it) affrighted my soul, so that I scarcely durst look upon them. These were not representations of men or of women, nor yet of beasts or birds, or of anything earthly—at least, in my knowledge—but phantastical; yet, notwithstanding, in some sense, real, signifying a meaning that I could not imagine; which made them the more affecting.

As to the man himself, I could never take to him, although he treated me kindly; for I was not able to shake off the dismal antipathy I at first conceived for him; and the shifting, spectral, black glancing of his eyes was always uneasy to me. Sometimes, however (and then I liked him better), there was that in him made me think him a great child; and, like a child, he abhorred to be in an unlighted place after dark fell, the only occasion when I saw him look angerly being when the steward delayed to bring the lantern to his cabin.

The other particular he took an interest in, and, as I may say, came to life (but it was a strange sort of life, more like a dream) was in the telling of tales, that were sufficiently outlandish and strange.

In all this time—I mean, in the first two or three weeks of our voyage—Mr. Huxtable kept his cabin for hours on end; and, when he was on deck, he used to stand still and silent beside the bulwarks, looking as in a muse upon the sea; else, paced up and down, with a heavy brow and a sad countenance, sometimes stroking of his beard; so that I durst not disturb him with my presence, or break in with any discourse upon his solemn cogitations.

CHAPTER VII

The Ghost Scare

It is convenient in this place to acquaint my readers, that, as I was not of age, nor skilled, at the time when these experiences happened to me, to take notice of many matters such as a knowing traveller or sailor, with his journal-book to furnish him, might set forth—points of navigation, winds, shifts of sail, bearing and distances of land, and the like: so I shall not attempt to indite a complete chronicle of my voyage, but express particularly only as my recollection serves: sufficient to relate, as best I can, such a difficult outlandish story, whereof the strangeness might stumble better capacities.

We had prosperous runs after we were gotten into the Trade wind, our ship sailing smooth in sunny warm weather (the nights delicious cool), and saw one of the Canary Islands (being the first land since Cape Finisterre) in the third week after we left the Channel, and on the next day, in the evening, we made the Island Teneriffe, where we designed to put in for some provisions.

We were to the N.W. of the Island, standing in for Oratavia, the wind being N.E.; but at supper the Captain seemed doubtful whether it had not been better to go for Santa Cruz, as being the better harbour, since, if the wind veered to the west, when we lay in the other road, we should not be able to ride. Mr. Falconer, being asked his opinion, answered: "When the wind is N.W., all ships must get up their anchors, or slip their cables, at Oratavia."

This put the Captain in a choler, which was no new thing with Mr. Falconer. "Why, this is Poll the Parrot," cried he and was running on with the like insulting expressions; but Mr. Huxtable interposed. "Yet Santa Cruz, you know, is an ill port also," said he, "if the N.E. wind grows stormy."

"That's true," said the Captain; "but Oratavia is worse with a westerly wind."

Hereupon, Mr. Falconer, who ate but little and drank less, asked leave to betake himself on deck; "With all my heart," said the Captain satirically.

"Well," said he, when he was gone, "we have heard tell how the Egyptians kept a skeleton at their banquets, but 'tis not everybody that hath a living one."

Mr. Huxtable misliking this manner of talk, presently rose up and went out, and I followed him, leaving the Captain venting his discontent in angry accents.

I was eager to see if the Pike was visible, which before had been hid with mist and clouds; and, looking up in the bright moonlight, I saw that the mist hung as an immense dim white curtain upon the land.

It rose high even unto the lofty clouds; but, on lifting up my eyes, I was amazed; for what I at first took to be a cloud reared in the form of a mountain-peak above the rest, I perceived to be, indeed, the summit of a great steep mountain, capped with snow; and I saw the ships standing at the base across the sea as little play-ships, so small they looked beneath the towering mountain.

"The Pike!" cried I, pointing with my finger.

"Ay," said Mr. Huxtable, "it hath a beautiful tapering top. It raises my clouded thoughts," said he, with a musing tone.

The light presently grew less, the moon being obscured with clouds. The mountain faded away from our ken; the little ships vanished.

"Alas, that it is gone!" said I.

"Nay," said he. "It is come! Let it be an image in your mind. When you did look upon it outwardly you could not see it there, in your mind; but now you see it. So in time of trouble when you are declined in spirit, or when you're dazzled with worldly pleasures, you shall conjure up the Pike of Teneriffe—yea, contemplate a still greater mountain in your thoughts, and so raise them up above the clouds. But 'tis late, and time you was abed. Come, be off with you, or you will be too heavy in the morning. I shall go to rest myself presently, and so will our ship also; for we shall lay by, and go in after sunrise."

So I went; but I could not sleep upon lying down, as I was wont to do; though the prospect of the mountain and Mr. Huxtable's noble admonition might well have composed my spirits. I lay broad awake; and soon my thoughts begun to turn as a wheel—nay, as a myriad wheels, spinning out strange imaginations. To stay the mind's engine is mighty work, compared with which the power to banish a single haunting thought (which, thanks to Mr. Huxtable's admonishing, I now possessed) is not so hard. The more I did endeavour to stop this endless coil, the worse it grew.

Thus, for hours, I lay restlessly turning, with fever and weariness nigh desperation; till, at last, a notion came into my head, that I had received a secret hint, or impression upon my mind, for some cause to go aloft.

This was much repugnant to me, both for a fear of Mr. Huxtable's censure if I should be discovered, and also for a fearful foreboding I felt of something unknown; so that I long strove with it, endeavouring to have conquered it, or to have banished it from my mind, hoping to have slid off to sleep in the midst. And so, anon, I might have done, for I begun to lie easier; but a rat run across my cabin floor, which effectually aroused me.

I rose up, and having put on my cloak, went fearfully forth into the dim 'tween decks (my cabin being near the round-house), designing to have gone on deck. I moved along, treading soft, but, coming to the foot of the hatchway, on a sudden, I stood, and quickly withdrew myself in a corner.

Somebody, or something, was approaching the way I came, making a shuffling, unsteady sound that set my heart a-drumming. I was comforted presently to see it was but a man (whatever I had feared), and a little ashamed of myself, too. As he came into the shaft of moonlight cast down the hatch, I saw it was Obadiah Moon, bearing a little pan, that, as I did observe, had held some fish. By his look, as well as by his staggering gait, twas plain he was drunk.

He mounted up the steps; and, after waiting until he was gone aloft, I did also. But there stood near the main-mast two or three of the watch in a chat; and, though they spoke but low, I heard something which made me willing, yet fearful, to have heard more; for it seemed to be concerning some strange matter, as of a haunting and apparition in the ship.

I endeavoured to have approached nearer, moving soft in the shadow cast by the sail, without being descried; but suddenly one of them, being the boatswain, saw me; and, pointing his finger at me, discovered me to the rest. They were all staring broad on me as if they were perfectly surprised and distraught with fear.

I perceived they took me for the ghost in my long black cloak, standing, as I did, between the shadow and the shine, and, after holding fixed in the posture of terror, they began to edge away all huddled under the poop. But, however, I spoke to them, asking what the matter was; which discovered their error. They appeared sensible they made but a foolish figure; especially the boatswain, that was somewhat of a great man among them; who, indeed, looked very rueful, while he stood gaping on me.

But, it came into my mind how odd a thing was this, that, after my taking Obadiah Moon for a spirit, they did immediately follow suit, thinking the like of me; my sense of which tickled me so (the more, I suppose, because I was so wrought up), I burst out a-laughing.

This was too much for the boatswain, who begun to curse and swear at me, supposing my laughter was at them. I assured him I was not laughing at him, or at any of them, but because of a notion that was come into my thoughts. Whereupon, "I wishes," said he fiercely, "as that you and your notions was sunk in the sea. And what brings you on deck, I wonder, in the middle of the night? Was you come to spy on us? What ha' we done, I wonder, to make you so suspicious? Belike there's a notion be come into your thoughts" (says he, mocking me) "that we be all rogues and pirates, and have some villainous design upon you. If you takes any more of your notions, I think I shall take such a notion as the effects on't will make you swallow your laughter down until it choke you."

The other handsomely applauded him, laughing and jeering at me after an extravagant manner; which, restoring him in his own conceit, put him in a better temper; but, following on his insulting speech, this stung me sufficiently.

"But what made you so ready to see a ghost?" said I, returning quick upon him. "To be sure you must have an uneasy conscience to be frightened at nothing!"

"Uneasy conscience?" cries he, stamping with his foot. "Damme! I'll wager I have a better conscience than some of you has aboard of this ship; else, how comes she to be haunted? It was never so before, or I should ha' known on't, having acquaintance with two of them that went to sea in her before, in her last voyage. And there's that aboard as ought not to be, nor aboard any craft on float the broad ocean. It an't arthly, and it an't nat'ral, and it an't wholesome, deny it who will! I says nought against the Captain, mark me!" (said he, hushing his voice). "No, nor against Mr. Huxtable neither, as is an honest gentleman and an hearty, that's true; and there's not a man of us but would serve him to the hazard of his life, and go with him to the world's end. He hath no hand in't, I warrants you! No, it an't him, and it an't the Captain; but there's some of us hath a shrewd notion who 'tis," said he, lifting his hand and pointing up behind him, where Mr. Falconer stood on the poop.

"And, I'll not be above telling you I meant no offence in what I says to you," said he with a milder tone. "But we was much troubled and perplexed in our thoughts what to think on't; and, as to being frighted at it, I be as bold as any; but a ghost is another thing."

"Maybe what the cook saw was nothing else but this young gentleman stirring down below," said one of the seamen. "Did you happen to go down in the fore-peak, young master?"

"No," said I, "but I saw Obadiah Moon coming that way. Perhaps he was this ghost."

I had scarce spoken when Obadiah himself appeared, stepping, with unsteady gait, along the main-deck. Next moment, oversetting as the ship rolled, he fell down all in a heap, and lay cursing and swearing. But, collecting himself presently, he rose up, after fetching some ineffectual endeavours, and stayed himself by gripping hold upon the gunnel. Thereupon, surveying us with his blear blinking eyes, "Hi! what's in the wind, messmates?" cried he. "What be this here perdition great consult under the moon?"

"We was discoursing of the ghost," said the seaman who had spoken to me.

"Ghost!" said Moon. "It's all moonshine. There an't no such thing. Feared on a ghost—was ye?

> *I'll sing ye a toon*
> *Of a ghost i' the moon.*"

So he run on, singing and swaggering in a tipsy bravado, rolling his eyes round on the men, that stood grinning on him, till, at last, he fixed them on me. Thereupon, letting go his hold, he came, staggering towards me across the deck.

"Here be a young gentleman of edication hath no fear of ghosts," said he. "Have ye, messmate?"

While he spoke, he thrust his face, all bloated with drinking, near to mine, his breath coming hot and villainous, so that I stepped some paces back to give him a wider berth. Whereupon, he asked if I thought he had the plague on him, since I seemed so frightened of him; and, with an horrible imprecation, "I never could a-bear with younkers aboard ship," said he. "Look 'e now, how I sarves 'em!"

With this, lowering grim, he pulled out his seaman's knife, and attempted to have unfastened the clasp; but, while he puzzled over it with his fumbling fingers, the boatswain snatched it smartly from his hand. "Let be, you drunken fool, you," said he, "and be off with you, or I'll give you a heave, you drunken swab!"

This brought him up quick; and he protested that he was but making a little merry and never intended me any harm, that he had taken a liking for me, and such maudlin stuff. He begun to move away under the boatswain's eye, his voice dwindling in tipsy complaints, but as he got further off, coming louder in curses. However, he had not gone far but he stumbled and fell upon the deck, and lay, making no endeavour to rise.

But, having thanked the boatswain for his timely intervening, I took the occasion to return to my cabin, shivering acold, on a sudden, in the night air.

While I went, I looked and saw Mr. Falconer, having taken no notice of this wild business, standing on the poop in a posture remarkably rigid; and his face, that was turned towards the sea, appearing more than ordinary pale in the moon, looked white and stiff like a mask.

I lay me down again; but, though after a manner I did sleep, 'twas worse than waking, being all troubled and broken with crazy dreams; wherein sometimes my grandfather, sometimes Obadiah played a part, and sometimes both in one, compacted into a sort of dreadful comic mime.

At last, some time after dawn, I dreamt that we were shipwrecked; and, waking up, I found that our ship indeed violently tossed and rolled, and that the day was cloudy. I suffered sorely, being my first knowledge of that miserable disorder of sea-sickness, and my head ached sufficiently. I was too sick and weak to rise when the hour came.

The bell rung to breakfast, and some time after Mr. Huxtable came in to see for me.

On learning what I ailed, he went and gave me to drink of some drug which made me easier, though still very queasy. I complained of the labouring of the ship, and asked him were we not yet nigh our port, when I might be conveyed ashore.

He told me that the wind having veered into the N.W., we were quite frustrated from going to Oratavia, and were beating round for the other port, adding for my comfort, that the sea would be less when we were on the east side of the island.

"Do you rest still," said he, wrapping another blanket, that he had brought, about me, "and keep yourself well covered. You have taken a chill, but the draught I have given you will allay your fever, and should compose you to sleep. Did you feel cold on deck last night?"

This took me by surprise; for I supposed his meaning to be when I was on deck after, and not before my going to rest.

"O!" said I, "did Mr. Falconer tell you?"

"Tell me," said he, "tell me what?"

"Why, about the ghost and Obadiah," said I.

"There, there, lad," said he, with a soothing accent. "You have been dreaming."

If I had not felt so weak, I think I had burst out a laughing, he did look so solemn; for I now perceived my error, and that, knowing nothing of the matter, he thought I roved in my mind.

So I made a shift to relate that crazy adventure with Obadiah and the rest; which, sitting down on a locker by my bedside, he heard with a grave countenance.

When I had ended, after pondering awhile, stroking of his beard, he desired me not to make any mention of it before the Captain, since he did think it better not to acquaint him, lest he should be too violently incensed against Mr. Falconer for behaving so negligently.

"Neither has he divulged the least word of it," said he; "for I had certainly heard of it if he had. I shall speak to him myself, and also examine how Obadiah provides himself with rum—whether pilfered from our store, or (what is more like) he did smuggle it aboard. This is the ghost that haunts the ship. This is the evil spirit we must exorcise."

I was not surprised by his resolution not to inform the Captain; for Mr. Falconer, of late, was become the chief target of his spleen, so that, furiously raging at him on every the least occasion, he seemed to spend his ammunition, our men getting off with scarce an angry word—yea, even that tardy carpenter!

Mr. Huxtable now left me, telling me that he would return when he was able, and, that, though I should feel much easier, I ought not to leave my cabin, but lie quiet and warm the rest of the day.

The motions of the ship were become less this while, and the potion I had drunk begun to work, soothing me into a quiet sleep.

When I awoke, the day was far spent, the porthole above my bed casting a comfortable soft light. The ship rolled but little, and with a different motion than before; and, when with an effort (for I continued very weakly), I sat up in my bed and looked out, I knew that we were come to our harbour. I beheld, at the distance of about half a mile over the sea (by how much the porthole did afford me prospect) a piece of a high steep land and some houses, being built of stone, that appeared very pleasant with their roofs of pantile all glowing in the sunset light.

Mr. Huxtable entered soon after to see if I was awake (having come in before while I slept); and, after enquiring how I did, and kindling my lamp, he sat him down by my bedside to entertain me with some news.

He said that we lay in the road at Santa Cruz, where we anchored soon after noon, that he had gone ashore in the long-boat to procure some of the provisions we had occasion for, and, that on the morrow, after filling our water casks (which could be done expeditiously in this place, in a sandy cove) it was proposed to refresh our men ashore.

He told me that he had spoken to Mr. Falconer, asking how he could possibly have behaved himself so negligent and remiss the last night; but that his answers were so extraordinary vague, he could make nothing of it.

"But I rather think," said he, that he was under some sort of demency, or ebbing fits of mind. I shall keep watch on him as much as I am able. The nights will grow warmer as we go along, and I shall move my bedding on deck.

For Obadiah, he lay in his bunk, having taken some hurt (as it should seem) in falling to the deck while drunk that night. He complained that his arm pained him; but what it ailed, Mr. Huxtable, though not unskilful in such matters, could not determine, and thought he might be pretending for some reason he had, perhaps fearing the Captain's censure on his drunkenness.

Be that how it might, for this occasion he said he would pass it over, bidding me as much as possible, henceforth, to keep out of this uncouth pirate's way.

Of the town, Santa Cruz, he told me it was but small, not above 200 houses, all two storeys high, with a convent and a church, and two forts to guard the road; but that three miles further up this rocky mountainous island, stood a town called Laguna from a great pond of fresh water (the word *Laguna* signifying in Spanish, pond or lake) that lies in a grassy plain at the back of the town, and that it was very handsome and delightful, with many fair buildings and gentlemen's houses, and among them convents, nunneries, and two churches, with high square steeples; the streets spacious, and, near the middle, a large parade. There are many goodly gardens of flowers and potherbs, set round with orange trees, limes and other fruits, that flourish exceedingly, since the town, standing on the brow of a plain, that is all open to the east, is seldom lacking for cooling and refreshing breezes from the Trade wind which is in these parts most commonly fair.

He told me also about Oratavia (being the chief seaport for trade) and many things beside concerning this island, and the other islands—as the various commodities they vend; some of which I have forgot, the rest omit as being not new, but related by travellers, nor necessary to my story.

CHAPTER VIII

Mr. Falconer Provides Obadiah

In taking his departure, Mr. Huxtable made me a promise, that, if I was recovered on the morrow, he would take me ashore to see the town, and, perhaps, climb the hill to Laguna. But, however, finding next morning, the fever yet upon me, he said that I was not in a condition to leave my cabin.

This was a shrewd disappointment to me; for I did feel strong enough, and I am sure that no traveller, returning to his own country after a long absence, could more eagerly expect to go ashore, than I did on this foreign island; which made my bed a burden, and the bright day of tedious long continuance.

Soon after wakening, I had heard much noise of stamping feet and voices calling on our deck, and it came again three or four hours after; being occasioned by the going and coming of our long-boat to fill our water. The second time, the commotion was longer drawn out, our men putting off first one boat and then another for their excursion ashore. Hearty loud and merry their voices came, with some dancing and tumbling (as it should seem), like boys out from school.

It passed, and all was silent, save those ordinary sounds of a ship on the sea—the clacking of blocks, and the like—while she lay slowly rolling and heaving at her anchor. Sometimes there came the shuffling sound of footsteps passing overhead; sometimes a hail from some ship that lay near us.

At last, about sunset, our holiday-makers returned, being as merry every whit, by the noise they made, as at their setting out. Soon after, Mr. Huxtable (having come in one of the boats) re-visited me, and declared, to my great content, that my pestilential fever was departed.

"Well, then," said I when he told me, "can I not immediately rise and go on deck?"

"Nay," answered he, with a solemn accent, and a terrible rueful countenance; "for I find you in another sort of fever."

"O la!" cried I, "what is that?"

"*A fever of impatience*," said he, laughing. "But I will not tease you, Will. I think you will take no harm if you put your cloak on."

So, having dressed myself quickly, I was in time to view the island before the light failed.

It rose up rocky and mountainous; which made the houses at the base appear the smaller and the more uniformly compact. They did look very pleasant, with their white walls and flat ruddy roofs, the small windows appearing in the sunset light to stare over the sea; two larger buildings—being the convents—and the church giving them countenance.

While I turned my eyes to observe a ship that lay near us (for there were several in the road, both large and small), glancing upon the main deck, I observed that Obadiah Moon was recovered from his ailment (whatever it was); and handsomely recovered too, as it should seem, for he stood in a vehement dispute with some of our men.

Whereupon, forgetful of Mr. Huxtable's admonishment to keep myself out of his way, I went to see what it was. Obadiah was in a regular passion presently, dancing up and down, and beating the air with his clenched fist; a spectacle of malignity to yoke (methought) with that admonitory object of foolishness which the Captain presented when he was in his rages. But there are those so weak-headed as rather to emulate a choleric constitution: let them choose whether they will be ridiculous like the Captain, or, like Obadiah—nay, like to my grandfather—venomously malign.

The occasion of Obadiah's ill-temper, as I learnt presently, was that one of his shipmates had failed to buy him a parcel of salted fish in the town, having agreed to perform this piece of service when he lay in his hammock unable to go ashore with the rest. But his wrath had been handsomely stirred up; for besides the inclination they had to hectoring or bear-bating—which is natural to Englishmen, especially the meaner sort—these seamen were somewhat merry, no doubt, from the entertainment they had found in some tippling-house ashore; nor was the Captain, or Mr. Huxtable, aloft to have moderated their wild spirits. Only Mr. Falconer stood on the poop, where I saw him appearing dark and gaunt against the crimson west, and the red lantern which was just kindled at the stern.

But while Obadiah stood brawling and raging, protesting that it was lack of fish for victual had made him sick (though he had complained to Mr. Huxtable of his arm), and that, if he had not expected to be provided by his messmate, he would have cast a fish-line over the gunnel and perhaps taken something, I observed Mr. Falconer was descending one of the poop-ladders, and wondered if he would, on this occasion, interpose; and, indeed, it was time that someone should; for, after thrusting his hand once and twice in his belt for his sailor's knife, the crazy furious creature now held it in his hand, while he looked glaring round on his mates, who, with altered faces, all stepped a pace or two back from him. Indeed, they were like to have been dangerously embroiled, had not the mate, having crossed the quarter-deck at this juncture, called to them.

"What is the matter?" said he, with his shrill lugubrious voice.

"Matter?" cried the boatswain warmly. "Matter and enough! Here be this crazy mad fellow a-proffering to murder us, and all for a matter (save the mark!) of a paltry parcel of fish. I near split my midriff with laughing till he pulled out his knife, the crazy loon!"

"Moon," said Mr. Falconer in his lugubrious voice, "Come hither! I have somewhat to say to you."

But Obadiah, turning about, with his knife in his hand, answered only with a villainous curse; while his small, dark, beady eyes appeared to gleam with a venomous lustre. The rest looked eager on, some grinning with such complacent and malicious curious countenances as conjured in my mind a different, yet like, spectacle; and I beheld, a moment, not those swarthy gazing seamen, but that crew of jeering school boys which stood tormenting me in Dr. Thompson's Academy.

But, fixing his eyes steadfastly on Obadiah, Mr. Falconer said, with the same tone:

"I have provided you your salted fish."

At this strange surprising utterance, the men at first stared, and then, looking one upon another, burst out laughing. But Obadiah was quite appeased; and, stepping toward Mr. Falconer, while he returned his knife to his belt, he said humbly:

"Thank'e, sir, thank'e. I be much beholden to you; and so is—and so" (said he, after a stop) "is my poor innards also."

"Ay, you makes game o' me, messmates," said he, turning himself about, "but, if you was plagued in your innards, as I am, after eating of flesh, you would be as fain, I'll warrant you, not to go a lacking for your victual of fish. Howbeit, I bears no ill-will, nor grudges, for all your laughter. And have ye took in good store for me, Mr. Falconer?"

"Store enough," answered the mate, standing gauntly up, while his eyes turned from side to side. "I shall give it to you when I go below."

Hereupon, he immediately betook himself away, stepping slow along the deck; while the men, gathering about Obadiah again, noisily uttered their surprise and laughter, recreating and sharpening their horny wit; which now he seemed not to mind, but took all in good part. But, as they had the less reason, on this account, to fear the sharp resentment of his knife, so, on the other side, he afforded them the less sport.

For a space they continued in it; while the sun set and darkness fell, a purple reflection tincturing the clouds above the lofty island with a kind of rueful and tragical brightness; which made a strange theatre for the comic scene. But soon, being weary of such a tractable object (the Captain in the meantime having come aloft), they desisted and begun to disperse.

Soon after, Mr. Huxtable, standing at the cabin door, called to me to come and get me in out of the night air, lest I should take cold after my distemper.

I passed in after him through the alley-way into the great cabin; whence he took me into the state-room, being on the starboard side, where he slept.

The first thing I remarked on entering in, was those pictures of a beautiful lady and a little child that I have described in Chapter IV, which were hung up by the wall over against his bed. He had a pen in his hand; and, upon a small table that stood beside his bed-head, there lay a manuscript book set open.

As he did not say anything concerning that extravagant business of Obadiah and our men, I concluded he had been too much occupied with writing to take notice of it. Neither did I speak of it, being unwilling he should know how carelessly I had slighted his bidding to keep myself out of Obadiah's way. I assured myself that it was but a trifling foolish matter, not worth his hearing; yet, when he told me, pointing with his finger to the manuscript-book, that he was just inditing his journal, in which he omitted nothing that fell out which was anyways beyond the ordinary, I was troubled with some reproaching doubts; which I conquered by telling myself that I would acquaint him some other time.

I was much taken with the form and look of his writing, which raised a desire of emulation in me. This was of serviceable effect to my narrative; for it brought me into the habitude of writing, causing me to set down, on some occasions, the substance of things that had passed.

I asked if he designed to publish his journal in a book, like Captain Dampier. He answered that he might consider of it if our voyage proved specially remarkable, or afforded any curious or profitable discoveries, but that this was not his principal end in writing, which was to keep his mind employed.

A mournful, afflicted look came into his eyes while he spoke this, recalling to my mind that sign of sorrow I read deep graven in his countenance at my first meeting with him in the kitchen of the farm. But, as if he would divert his thoughts from some lamentable topic, he immediately begun a discourse on the uses and instruction of writing, which he called *the pastime of noble minds*. "For ordinary men," said he, "like to children with their playthings, are busied with material things; but the writer with spiritual things."

Thus the time passed until supper. Rising up at the sound of the bell, Mr. Huxtable put his journal-book away in a drawer, together with some papers that he had left upon his locker (for he was a man that could not endure any disorder, and liked to have all things trim and handsome about him); and we went and sat down with the Captain and Mr. Falconer, who were just entered in.

'Twas but a dull supper-party: Mr. Huxtable holding silent most part of the time, with a heavy brow and a brooding mind; and, though once and twice he endeavoured to rouse himself and essayed a merry word, 'twas but *a flash in the pan* (as the saying is); Mr. Falconer, as usual, speaking but in brief replies; and the Captain was occupied sufficiently with the diligence of eating and drinking. Anon, however, he begun to discourse of his grand acquaintance and relations (as he thought them), his wonted topic whenever he found, or could make a way, to wind into it; as thus:

The Captain (setting down his cup and turning his head affably towards Mr. Huxtable): "Sir, I was very sorry not to go ashore with you today, for I should have had the honour to present you to the Governor."

Mr. Huxtable: "I did not know, sir, that you were acquainted with the Governor."

The Captain: "Nay, sir, I am not myself acquainted with him; but my cousin is his familiar friend, and is accustomed to dine with him whenever his ship lies off the town."

Mr. Huxtable: "Well, sir, I should have been glad to have pleasured you by waiting upon the Governor with you."

The Captain (warmly): "Pleasured me, sir! *Pleasured me*, say you? Sir, give me leave, I do always humbly endeavour to follow a precept of my ingenious kinsman, Mr. William Andrews, Justice of the Peace for the County of Dorset, who, as possibly you are aware, is the author of a volume of apophthegms. *He that doth acknowledge no one better than himself* (says he) *can scarce know anybody worse*, and a Governor is a Governor, by my estimation."

Mr. Huxtable: "Ay, sir, very like."

This answer of Mr. Huxtable, uttered, as it was, with a careless, listless accent, put the Captain into a fuming choler; which he vented obliquely upon Mr. Falconer, with some contemptuous expressions glancing on his conduct of our men, implying that the chief reason for his not going ashore was, that, if the Governor had asked him to sup with him (as, in all likelihood, as he supposed, he would have done), he should have been absent when our men returned on board the ship, and then, in the merry temper they were in after regaling themselves ashore, they might have occasioned some disorder.

But Mr. Huxtable replied not at all to this; and the mate, rising from his chair after his vacant manner, with that strange, black, slant shifting of his eyes, betook himself from the cabin.

Neither was the discourse, thus fallen in the midst, picked up; for Mr. Huxtable now rose also, plucking me by the arm; and I followed him out, leaving the Captain to his wine, sipping glum.

CHAPTER IX

Some Remarkable Adventures: The Author Arrives at Pernambuc

The wind rose in the night, blowing from the N.E. and, growing stormy, made our berth dangerous. Early in the morning, accordingly, all things being now in readiness for our departure, we sailed, with a great stress in weighing anchor, hastening out all we could in a great tumbling sea.

The Captain designed next for Pernambuc; and we ran away right afore the wind (being the N.E. Trade), at the rate of nine or ten miles an hour, all that day and night; and, though it slackened on the day following, 'twas but to become the more constant, like a runner fallen into a steady pace: so, with brisk gales and fair weather, we went on towards the south-west.

In this time I was much diverted by the flying-fish, that came fluttering like birds (indeed they looked much like swallows) about our bows, and at night about our poop-lantern.* The first time I saw them, there came a strange remote, and yet, nevertheless, lively recollection into my mind, as if I had seen them afore; and perhaps I had, when

---

* We did also hang out lanterns to take them (MS. annotation).

(as I have related in Chapter I) in my early childhood I was aboard my father's ship in his West India voyages.

Sometimes one or two fell on our deck, and were eagerly taken by our men; for they are firm, well-tasted fish, much resembling dry herring. Once I observed Obadiah to take up one of them, that, unperceived by the rest, had gotten under the long-boat, and conceal it behind him; and, having stayed where he was until the deck was clear, he did bear it off instead of delivering it to the cook, as he ought to have done; as if the barbarous creature was willing to devour it undressed. I acquainted Mr. Huxtable with this uncouth particular; but he only laughed, saying that Obadiah had sure been born under the sign *Pisces*.

Five or six days after our departure from Santa Cruz, we passed by the Cape de Verde Islands at the instance of about three leagues; but night was fallen, and all we saw was the flames issuing from the top of the island of Fogo, being a volcano. I did view the spectacle (Mr. Huxtable having allowed me to stay up to see it) with wonder and delight, and a kind of awe, my imagination being ever powerfully taken by a volcano, and wished that the mountain itself had been visible. But Mr. Huxtable, when I imparted to him my desire, told me, that, if it had been, the flames, which by night may be seen a great way off at sea, would not have been visible.

"And who shall tell," added he, "that it is not likewise with our souls? which are themselves a kind of volcanoes and islands. Let your thoughts" (said he solemnly), "feed on such pure and such combustible fuel as engenders not vapours nor sulphurous smoke, that might well appear by day, but ethereal flames."

In all this time—I mean, since our departure from Santa Cruz— our men had an easy life: no pulling and dragging of the yards; for days on end, scarce need to stir a brace.

They had idled the time away, casting dice, and the like; but Mr. Huxtable, to amuse and raise their thoughts, often discoursed with them in a company on the main-deck; and 'twas really surprising how apt he found some of them, holding dialogues with them, as it were a Socrates at sea.

Not all, however, attended these discourses; and some (of whom was Obadiah) did covertly scoff, and, like foolish schoolboys, had turned all to laughter if they had dared. Sometimes that ancient seaman whom I have told you of, left his pious reading and sat him down in the company, looking attentively and gravely on, with his gentle shining gaze like a benediction.

As for me, I own, I made but an infrequent auditor, being drawn more powerfully elsewhere; for Mr. Falconer rigged his little ships, squatted down under the break of the poop, and I delighted to observe him. Nay, he told me wonderful strange tales while I sat by his side; which seemed always to be of others' adventures, never of his; nor did he ever relate any passage of his life's history. He spake but as a voice in the air; which, in one way, as if they were told by their actors, did make his narratives the more enthralling to me; as if I listened to a voice within me that yet proceeded from without.

Once he told me there's an island that lies near submerged in the sea, and that strange things might befall a ship that happened to be near in those parts. But, upon my asking where it was, and what manner of things, he answered only that they were past understanding, and would tell me no more, though I did urge him, save that there shined an extraordinary strange light.

"Why, have you seen it?" said I.

"If I had seen it," said he, "I should not be here. Yet I have seen it in part, and am never the same after. Never the same. Ha!"

He spoke this with a muttering low tone of voice, that dwindled with a ghostly sound; and immediately after, he sunk into a kind of absent fit, glaring dolefully with a look like a kind of gleaming blindness in his eyes, that kept continually turning casting their slant black glitter in the sun.

It gave me a horrible scare. But he soon recovered himself; and thereupon besought me not to tell Mr. Huxtable, or the Captain, what he had said, lest they should account him to be mad.

"Nay, 'tis but a sailor's tale," said he. "I could relate many such wonderful outlandish stories, and so I will if you pass me your word you will not blab."

His wild aspect and the queer tones of his voice affected me with oddly compounded feelings—as pity and wonder and a kind of ghostly dread; and my readers may conceive how such experiences as this conduced to render him phantastical, not to say downright affrighting, in my thoughts and imaginations, so that he was become sometimes as a kind of substantial spectre and (in a manner of expression) daylight ghost unto me.

Now, to hark back to Mr. Huxtable and his discourses to our men: I have told you that some derided them, and they, indeed, were abetted secretly therein by no less a person than the Captain himself, holding that Mr. Huxtable went too much out of his station to be so familiar with common seamen.

This was soon divulged to me in some passages between the Captain and Mr. Huxtable. It was the sole occasion when I saw my worthy patron in anger, and it not a little served to establish his authority over the Captain. It happened in the cabin after dinner; and, as recollection serves me, I set it down:

"I venture, sir," said the Captain, "to remark upon something I have often wondered at—I mean, that remarkable condescension you show towards our men in discoursing with 'em on deck, as you are accustomed to do."

I thought this very handsome, and was the more surprised, therefore, when Mr. Huxtable answered, as he did, somewhat haughty and satirical.

"I thank you," said he; "although, I own, I do not see any great condescension in it. I do but endeavour a little to raise their thoughts. I think I ought rather to compliment you in discovering so much sensibility as to consider it condescending."

"Nay, sir," said the Captain, with a mincing accent, "I shall hold to my opinion of it, by your leave; although, I protest, the profit of our men in what you say to them is really beyond estimation."

Upon this, Mr. Huxtable turned sharply in his chair, while an angry flush came over his face.

"You own, do you?" said he, with a low stern tone, "that it's profitable to them. It cannot but appear the stranger, then, that you should endeavour, as you do, as much as possibly you can, to dash and defeat the effects by thrusting in, when I am gone, your satirical and sneering comments! How, sir?" cried he, with a voice like crashing thunder, "have you dared?"

But the Captain, being quite subdued by this sudden astonishing rebuke, answered not a word; and Mr. Huxtable rose up presently, and betook himself out on the deck.

Being past the Cape de Verde Islands, we steered more easterly, and soon met with a great rippling sea, which, as the Captain told us, was caused by a strong current setting against the wind; and with many other such in the next six or seven days. In this time we saw some sharks and benitoes.

Sometimes the wind whiffled about, sunk, leaving us becalmed, and sprung up afresh; which gave our men work enough. Sometimes lowering clouds darkened the seascape; and then, indeed, the windows of heaven were opened; for the rain fell as if the swollen sea was another Flood. Sometimes there came a roaring tornado.

As we got near the equator, we had pretty fair weather, with some small winds and calms. During the calms, some of our men, especially Obadiah, took some fishes, having their lines slung over the gunnel. But I disliked the barbarous appearance of this sport, and always have. Accordingly, I was the less diverted from my book to observe it (for Mr. Huxtable began to enter me in the rudiments of the Latin tongue); though I often stood to view the porpoises, of which a great many came swimming past, turning quickly in the breaching waves as if they did play before us.

Now, in regard to these porpoises, hear a strange story. One of our men, called Merry Jack, struck one of them with a fizgig. Whereupon, the carpenter's mate, that stood near him, uttered a kind of doleful cry, and, "Farewell, Jack," said he; "for you're not long for this world, that's true."

"Why, what do you mean?" said Merry Jack, leaving to haul in the porpoise, that lay violently bending and unbending on the dart, while the waves turned red with its blood. "How not long for this world? I be hale enough."

"Very like you be," returned the other; "but you won't be for long. Don't you know that he who strikes a porpoise, strikes through the heart in his own body?"

This gave him such a scare, he let the porpoise go, fizgig and all.

"But I have seen men strike porpoises afore," said he, with a small faltering voice.

"Very like you have," said the carpenter's mate, returning quickly upon him; "but have you seen them take any?"

"No," said Merry Jack, halting in his speech. "No, messmate, I can't recollect as I have. But I have let this-here porpoise go free."

"Let him go free, have you?" said his mate scornfully, while he pointed to the sea; where the porpoise, having ceased to struggle and now (as it should seem) quite dead, appeared a moment just sinking beneath the waves. "So shall you go free, I warrants you, when we ha' let go your dead carcass sinking down!"

"But I did strike un unwitting and in ignorance," said the poor man, fetching his last endeavour. "Sure, it should avail if I struck un in ignorance!"

"Well, I hope it may; but I'ld not lean on such a sorry staff if I was you. But come, Jack" (said this ruthless comforter), "a sailor's life an't as merry as a porpoise's, I warrants you! so where's the sorrow if it happen as it will, and you slips your cable and goes away from this port of arthly trouble?"

So saying, he turned, and, with a countenance more droll than befittingly serious, betook himself away; while Merry Jack, leaning with his back against the bulwarks and his head sunk upon his breast, appeared to yield himself to the very drench and abysm of despair.

I was sorry for the woebegone creature; and, stepping to him, endeavoured to have comforted him by reasoning with him and showing him his error in giving any credence to such a piece of foolish superstition as this was; but he said shortly, that I, being but a younker, knew nothing at all. When I told him that Mr. Huxtable would certainly confirm what I said, he answered that Mr. Huxtable had not lived a seafaring life, as he had, and that all his learning and all his wisdom was not able to weigh in the scales against actual experience.

"Call it superstition, or by what long name you will," said he, with a passionate burst, "and veer out your cable to the better end, 'tis all one. I have seen what I have seen; and the sea will perform his matters."

So, seeing that he would be rid of me, I went away, leaving him in a deep dump. On acquainting Mr. Huxtable, as I did as soon as I found occasion, he said that he would touch upon these foolish superstitions in his next discourse to our men.

This, no doubt, had been on the morrow if the calm had held, but the wind, springing up in the night, blew an uncertain small gale all that day, which kept our men pretty busy handing the sails, so that there was no opportunity.

On the day following, we crossed the line; and, the small inconstant gale continuing, crept slowly southward against a great swell out of the S.E., the Captain taking every occasion of an east wind, though it blew but in a flurry, to get beyond this region of uncertain winds, calms, rains, and tornadoes; which, besides retarding our course, might endanger sickness among our men.

In the preventing as much as possible such sickness, care was ever had of Mr. Huxtable in rainy weather that our men shifted themselves when wet, having, in this respect, the same experience with them, as Captain Dampier tells us he had with his own men; for, what the heat of the weather and their continual labours, and the natural carelessness of such people, they were too lazily propense to lie down in their hammocks in their drenched or dank clothes.

Thus was Mr. Huxtable's discourse procrastinated. But as, in the meantime, the poor credulous man apparently languished under a settled despondency and despair, he told me he would take an occasion to speak with him, lest he should either desperately do himself a mischief, or else grieve himself to death, and so (which is no unlikely issue in such cases) bring along that selfsame calamity whereof he was in dread.

Now, as was afterward discovered, the carpenter's mate who had frightened the poor man with this porpoise story, was one that had a *crotchet* (as it is called), which was an extravagant overweening regard for animals, especially fishes and all manner of sea-beasts—in the sense that he did esteem them above human kind. It is extremely probable, therefore, that he invented the superstition himself, on purpose to avenge that murdering of the porpoise.

Be this what it will, the sea itself, by what odd working of the law, or *no-law* of contingency, or coincidence, which, on some occasions, is so remarkable in things, in this sad incident seemed also to play his prank. For, while Mr. Huxtable was speaking to the man, being the third day, in the morning, after we crossed the equator, and, with gentle soothing words and persuasive reasons fit for his understanding, began a little to work upon his stubborn dejectedness, what should happen, but that, just as he uttered the word, the dead carcass of a porpoise did appear driving in the waves near the side; which put a period to Mr. Huxtable's endeavour. Nay, to end my tale, which is sufficiently dismal, the man fell sick the very next day, having, as Mr. Huxtable thought, taken a chill in the night; and, so low now was his bodily strength declined, 'twas not of power to resist, so that, despite all the care and remedies that could be used with him, he continually sunk, and lived not above three days after.

My readers, perhaps, will think this but a foolish story, scarce worth the setting down. Nevertheless, the experience of such superstitious credulity, and its evil consequence, was very exemplary to my understanding and a great confirmation of Mr. Huxtable's counsels, admonishing me that they who steer their course by the logic stars are not unwise, regarding monsters and marvels, whether old or new, as mere spectacles in the heavens, not to be steered by, nor unreasonably observed. Not that I deny there be hidden causes in things, undiscovered laws, occasioning prodigies (so thought), which in times to come, perhaps, will be intelligibly discerned; and of this my narrative in the sequel bears good witness.

Something in this sense I did write in a small manuscript book that I had made; and showed it, not without diffidence, to Mr. Huxtable; which, with a countenance of the utmost gravity (though, methought, there was a sort of smiling appearance in his eyes), he greatly commended.

"And, to conclude pithily," said he, "you might add, that, although there's a constellation called the *Crab*, we have yet to learn of a *Porpoise*!"

Asking the reader's pardon for this digression, I proceed.

The calms and shiftings of winds which we met with in crossing the line, though to be expected by any experienced seaman, were very provoking to our men's tempers: much more to the Captain's, hot and testy, as any the least stop, or delay, in our course always made him; but his continual fault-finding with the mate (if Mr. Huxtable was not by) seemed rather amusing to the on-lookers than afflicting to his object; in which respect it might be accounted somewhat commodious. 'Twas in vain the Captain's bewailing himself to Mr. Huxtable; for, if he did, he answered that it was only what any seafaring man might expect in crossing the equator; to which the Captain could but assent, unless he would be ridiculous.

But, however burthensome and vexatious to everybody else on our ship this inconstant season may have been, 'twas full of novel and affrighting experiences to me: whether in a hot sultry calm our ship rolled heavily in sluggard surges, or a tornado came roaring over the sea. If 'chance a fierce flurry surprised us before our men had time to take in enough sail, it set us heeling with our lee ports under, leaving sometimes a strong constant wind, and we ran away right afore it at ten or twelve knots, casting a foaming wave at our bows.

The dazzling gaudy colours I often saw at sunset struck my soul with admiration; for in the parts about the equator they are exceeding glowing and grand; and, if I attempted to describe such a wonderful enthrilling phenomenon, I should be obliged to invoke (if that were not profane) the aid of some pagan muse and be barbarically poetical: to tell you that the heavens had put on their Tyrian and flaming robes to celebrate the festival of the dying Sun; while, reared up before them in their vestments of many glowing hues of purple and cinnamon, yellow, green, and blue, the spent and phantastical shaped clouds were piled as a sacrifice upon the altar, tier upon tier, above the western horizon.

Likewise also of the extreme bright shining of the moon; comparable to Venus' dazzling charm. But to tell of the stars in their multitude, that hung like lamps of living gold, would need a higher mood, above mythological imaginations.

Being now come to about three degrees south of the line, we had again a brisk constant wind from the N.E., which carried us to the coast of Brazil.

'Twas early in the morning when we sailed round Cape St. Augustine, being the easternmost promontory; and, after standing in traverse on the south side, we anchored among many other ships, both great and small (being the ordinary riding-ground of the port), two or three leagues from Pernambuc.

The weather was very fair; as it had been since we met with the N.E. wind; and, under the clear spaces of the sky, the sea appeared extraordinary transparent and bright, like crystal shot with flame.

I looked with longing upon the land; that rose up, beyond some low hills, mountainous high, but having a pleasant and gracious aspect, not harsh and stern, being all chequered with woods and savannahs. By the sea-side stood some small houses, about the size of our English cottages, being, as I suppose, fishermen's dwellings; but, in the distance, towards the south, I could see the town, that lay about a mile from the shore, looking very handsome and considerable, with the walls of many great buildings shining in the sun exceeding white, like bleached bone. Very eagerly I expected to go ashore, especially after being frustrated at Santa Cruz; and Mr. Huxtable said that he would take me with him when he went after noon.

He told me that he did not design to make any long stay at this port, since we had already stocked ourselves at Santa Cruz, but only one day to fill our water, and buy some provisions as fruits, especially limes and oranges, which here were very abundant. In the meantime, between the going and returning of our boats, our men should refresh themselves ashore.

CHAPTER X

Violent Strange Behaviour of Obadiah: Pernambuc Described

It was convenient that the Captain, having some acquaintance with Portuguese, should go ashore to treat with the merchants himself in the providing what we wanted, there being, as he was credibly informed, few or no Englishmen in the port; since the European trade was in Portuguese vessels, as were those that lay with us in the road.

Soon after he had gone in his boat, there appeared some very odd clumsy-looking craft, which came towards us, being contrived of several logs fastened side by side, with one mast or two, carrying large sails. In each of them sat two men, one at either end.

These were fishermen, being very swarthy, slovenly dressed, and of a sort of jocose villainous cast of countenance; and, one of their craft coming aboard of us, Mr. Huxtable bought some fish, which was in a basket hanging up at the mast. Thereupon, after delivering the fish to the steward, he betook himself aft, to go to his cabin, bidding me, while he went, to acquaint him as soon as I saw the Captain's boat returning, that he might have timely notice to break off his work and make ready to go ashore; when he would take me with him to see the town.

No sooner his back was turned, but Obadiah stepped to the gangway, where the log-boat was preparing to depart, and bought, in haste, the residue of the fish, tossing on the deck, with careless prodigality in requital, a gold coin; whereupon, he stepped stealthily forward, with his arm full, glancing his eyes on me, with a sullen angry look; but was not gotten above a few paces when the boatswain, standing near the break of the poop, called to him to stand.

"Hi! you fish-glutton," cried he, "come you hither; I spied you, you greedy cormorant! I have some work for you."

But Obadiah did but make the more speed; upon which, the boatswain, flying into a rage, started off in pursuit, bawling to some of our men, that chanced to be in Obadiah's way, to lay hold on him. But he, charging headlong in between them, set them staggering on either side, some of his fish falling scattered with the shock. Nevertheless, two of them being thoroughly enraged at this rough dealing, quickly recovering themselves, though they could not stop him, availed to fob him off from 'scaping down the hatchway. They, thereupon, joined in the pursuit with the rest, the boatswain holloing them on; and a fair course they had around the deck; till, at length, apprehended—or rather, tripped up by one that stood in wait for him—Obadiah was delivered to the boatswain.

Others of our men, who had looked on, stood almost splitting their sides with laughing; which not a little increased the boatswain's wrath.

He, having received charge to repair some damage occasioned to our yards and rigging by the stormy winds, was going to muster his men, among whom was Obadiah, to begin this work forthwith; and he railed on the miserable captive that had hindered him, shaking his fist in his face, with the most insulting epithets. Not less incensed was Obadiah himself, who stood muttering villainous and vile recriminations, with a wretched remnant of his fish dangling in his hand.

Having spended thus the ammunition of his spleen, the boatswain now, with summary words, dispersed those standing round, by sending them about their business, being chiefly aloft in the yards and rigging. But Obadiah he set to mending of a rent topsail on the deck; where, squatting down with the canvas spread over his knees, he begun to ply his sail-needle after a vicious, jerking manner. Once I saw him glance his eyes up at the boatswain with a singular look, while his lip writhed in a sort of covert and despiteful laughter. I was not near enough to hear any sound of speech; yet I seemed to myself to hear him say, even more lively than if I had heard it actually in words, that he would be even with the boatswain and this in such fashion as he could never expect.

One of our men, descending from the masts, cast out a flouting jest, derisively commenting upon that paltry remnant of Obadiah's fish, that he had set down by his side, enquiring if he designed to make it the daintier morsel by broiling it in the sun, that it might compensate by excellence what it wanted in bulk.

In the same time, another attempted to have taken it from him. But, as if he had expected such a practic jest and had his answer pat—which was his knife—he did return so smart an answer that the jester could not but own (though not with laughter) that it had some point.

And, "Here be a small spare slip of one of your fingers," said he, flourishing his bloody knife. "If you meddles with my fish again, I'll carve the whole joint. D'you see this knife, messmates?" said he, grinning broad. "This knife's an old knife, a good knife; hath known a mort of service. Come on, ye dogs! will you barter flesh for good fish?"

While he spoke, Obadiah looked really like a fiend. A wild beast is but a brute creature, however fierce and terrible it may be; but, when a man is subdued unnaturally to the brutish element, he is neither man nor beast, but demoniac, like this vile miscreant, whose knife, in an horrible phantasy, seemed (as it were) to be a part and extension of his hand that held it, a steel and bloodstained claw. But, Obadiah, indeed, with his smooth, round, grinning, malign face, appeared like a foolish and dreadful mime.

Those two seamen recoiled from him, and, without more parley, went their ways: the one that had played that prank on him, betaking himself below to bind his wound, that bled sufficiently; the other returning to his work on the main-mast.

Soon after, comes the boatswain, having been absent this while; and, stepping, as it chanced, just in the track of the droppings of blood upon the deck, he asked me what it was, in the same time glancing his eyes at Obadiah, who was just returning his knife to his belt. I told him that Obadiah had wounded one of our men; and, Mr. Falconer being now come aloft, without waiting to hear any more, he went running to the quarter-deck where he stood, and called out, after an impetuous angry manner, that Obadiah was become a mutinous, dangerous madman, desiring that he would immediately come and deal with him.

Mr. Falconer immediately went with him; and, stepping to Obadiah, who now wrought steadily with his needle, he demanded what answer he could make to the boatswain's accusation of his being so troublesomely and violently turbulent.

Obadiah replied, with a mild tone and humble demeanour, that, as to his not stopping when the boatswain called to him, he did but intend to stow away the fish he had bought of the Portuguese fishermen, and would have returned forthwith to have done the boatswain's bidding; and, as to wounding the man, he had tried to snatch away the sole fish that was left him.

"Howsoever," added he, "I do own and confess that I be guilty and much amiss, and I be ready to suffer my punishment, even though it should be so heavy as the forfeiting of my going ashore with the rest."

While he uttered the conclusion of this speech, which I thought very odd, I observed he looked at Mr. Falconer extraordinary hard; and, at the end, to my astonishment, he winked distinctly with his eye; immediately glossing this familiar insolent act by closing and opening his eyes twice and thrice, exclaiming:

"Bless us! begging of your pardon, how the glare do plague my poor eyes!"

"Pity 'tis it don't plague your tongue also," said the boatswain testily. "If I was the Captain, I would serve you according to the tenor of your words and debar you from going ashore."

"Nay," said Mr. Falconer, with a violent loud tone, that was much unlike his usual manner of speaking, "that were indeed fitting, bos'n; and I will go bail that the Captain will be in the same opinion; for I do intend to acquaint him with these disorders. You may, therefore, confidently expect to see this punishment performed."

Obadiah began to cry out on this, protesting that it was very hard, and the like; while the boatswain stood scratching of his head, with a dubious and troubled countenance; for he was rather hastily choleric by nature, than actually severe, and would threaten worse than he did intend.

"Well, the wounding was no great matter," said he, "and he had received provocation, that's true! And, seeing as the man is penitent,—"

"Say no more, and let be!" said Mr. Falconer, abridging him.

With this, which he spoke in his usual lugubrious tone, he shortly turned away, and stepped, after his slow and listless manner, towards the quarter-deck, leaving us amazed at his conduct.

"Well, who could have thought?" said the boatswain, staring after him.

Thereupon, glancing round and spying some of our men standing by the bulwarks curiously observing him, he turned sharply on his heel, and betook himself forward. Obadiah, who, since Mr. Falconer had finished speaking, sat intent over his work (as it should seem), as if the matter concerned not him at all, looked up, letting fall his needle; and, turning his eyes towards the departing boatswain, he set his thumb to his nose and spread forth his fingers, grimacing with derision.

This odd scene not a little raised my curiosity; and, putting together Mr. Falconer's obliging Obadiah by purveying him some fish on that occasion when we lay off Santa Cruz, and the understanding and compliance that there seemed to be between them in the matter of the *punishment* (Obadiah appearing, for some reason he had, to be unwilling to go ashore), I sharply conjectured there was something in it of concernment to our voyage—I mean, Mr. Huxtable's adventure—whatever that might be.

Pluming myself upon this acute perception (as I thought it), I was immediately going to acquaint Mr. Huxtable; but stopped on the way, bethinking myself that I should be too impetuous to break in upon him at his work. I stood looking landward over the sea, idly expecting to see the Captain's boat returning, although I knew it could not yet be for some hours. I saw two or three small craft lading or unlading beside the shore, and a great ship careening—that is, being purged by fire of limpets and the like incumbrances—the smoke rising in white puffs in the clear air. After a while, the boatswain blew his whistle to muster the long-boat's crew; and soon they pulled away, with our empty jars aboard, to fill our water.

At last, a little after noon, I spied the Captain's boat, and went to acquaint Mr. Huxtable. The door of his cabin, standing open, I passed within and saw him seated at his desk, having his papers set out before him and a pen in his hand. At my entry, he turned his head and looked upon me with a severe countenance and a staring eye; which, thinking he was in anger, quite confounded me, and I was not a little comforted when, in the next moment, his look changing, showed me that he was but roving in his thoughts.

Having performed my errand, I went on to tell him about Obadiah and the boatswain, and Mr. Falconer's odd conduct; nor did he laugh at my suspicions, which I told him, of there being some secret understanding between Obadiah and Mr. Falconer, as, while I was speaking, I was apprehensive he might do, but heard all with a countenance of the deepest gravity, which, as appeared by the look in his eyes, was in no sort affected.

"Well," said he when I had ended, "you have done well in acquainting me with this. Do you continue to keep your eyes open for anything else that may look strangely, but do not speak of it to anybody, only to me."

The hour of dinner was struck presently; and, as soon as we were sat down, and the Captain had carved the beef, he, being in spirits, began to entertain us with relating how he had waited on the Governor, what a fine house he dwelt in, and the handsome compliments he had made him: "In no article differing" (said he) "than if I had been the captain of a King's ship, or, indeed, for that matter, a member of the English peerage."

This was, methought, but to angle for another compliment; in which Mr. Huxtable civilly indulged him.

"Nay, sir," said he, "I think it is no marvel though he did; for, you know, you have had some more than ordinary acquaintance with persons of quality, and may be conceived to have taken some colour from their coat."

"Do you think so?" says the Captain, forgetting to eat, and leaning forward with a flush on his face.

"I think so indeed," answered Mr. Huxtable. "Do not we emulate where we sedulously love?"

But, seeing the Captain looking somewhat doubtful and suspicious, he added:

"Sir, I do not mean only in the outward appearance. We really take on ourselves the nature of that which we sincerely imitate, so we be not actuated by nothing but vanity. You say that the Governor has a large house. Did you observe if it was as fine within? I have heard that the Spanish and Portuguese in these parts abroad do affect to have large houses, but are little curious about their furniture, or having them handsome within."

"He had some brave pictures," answered the Captain in brief; and seemed to brood in his mind while he ate, as if Mr. Huxtable's remarks had provided him with some matter for cogitation.

CHAPTER XI

The Author Ashore at Pernambuc

After dinner, Mr. Huxtable took me ashore, as he had promised to do; but, not to delay my story with any large or particular descriptions (which, indeed, I am not able to furnish), I shall relate only such matters as adhere in my recollection.

First, the town of Pernambuc is of considerable size: the principal streets are large; the houses two or three storeys high, strongly built of stone, with massy thick walls, and covered with pantile, some having balconies. There are some considerable buildings, of which (as the Captain had told us) the Governor's house stood very conspicuous; but chiefly churches and convents, which, with the sound of their bells, seemed to dominate the town, as things papal use to do. The high towers appeared to cast their ecclesiastical and monastical shadows across the small paving-stones of the streets; and hooded friars—black, white, and grey—passed as ghostly visitants among the people. I observed that the soldiers were dressed in brown linen. By far the most in number were the black shoremen being busied either in quality of porters, carrying goods to or from the landing-place, or serving in the shops. Some went running beside their masters, riding on horseback; others bore them in hammocks.

These hammocks, or palanquins, are a pretty sight. They are carried on the shoulders of two bearers by the means of a long pole, and are made of cotton, mostly blue. A covering comes over the pole quite encurtaining the person thus carried, unless he pleases to put it by, and then you shall see him reposing, having pillows for his head, sometimes saluting his acquaintances whom he meets in the streets.

I observed two of these palanquins at a standstill alongside of each other, those who were within leisurely conversing in a sitting posture, being supported by their pillows, with their legs hanging out over one side. These were stout bulky Portuguese, or Spaniards (I know not which), but their carriers were eased of bearing them up; being performed by strong staves, upon which the pole of the hammock rested, one at each end, having a sharp iron at the foot sticking fast in the ground. They did stand remarkably still and composed, while their masters talked, lifting their arms and hands. You might have fancied them to be figures carved out of ebony.

There were gardens both within and in the outer parts of the town, planted with fruit trees—especially oranges and limes—flowers, herbs, and saladings; among which I observed cabbages, turnips, and onions. Here were also (as Mr. Huxtable discovered to me) various drugs—as sassafras, snake-root, and physick-nuts. Here I saw some comely and curious trees, of which one, having great, broad, slab leaves, brought to my recollection a picture that hung in my grandfather's parlour of a scene in the Garden of Eden.

Many fowls frequented these gardens, especially turtle-doves and pigeons; and I saw a gaudy parrot, that, from its perch on one of the topmost branches, tore at the leaves, screeching as if it was in a mad fury.

As to fruits, Mr. Huxtable told me, that, if the season of the year had not been so late (for 'twas now late autumn), I had seen in this town a surprising great diversity, such as he believed there was not in the world another town or country could show the like: that, besides abundance of oranges, limes, grapes, plums, melons, pineapples, pomegranates, plantains, and bonanoes, there were yet some others which are not met with in other places; and, indeed, there was still some left, and, I saw them in the shops: being one, round and green, as big as a small orange; another, a small red fruit the size of a cherry; it is flat on one side, and hath protuberant ridges.

Both are pleasant refreshing fruits (for we did taste of them), though somewhat tart on the tongue.

In the most eminent places of the town, there are parades, which, with the gardens, do make it the more handsome and spacious. While we walked along one of these, we saw two of our men in company with black women, being a little in advance of us. Upon one of them glancing round his eyes and spying us, we observed they mended their pace; and, arriving the end of the parade, they betook themselves quickly into a narrow side-street, or alley-way; so that we saw them no more.

This, as plainly appeared from his demeanour, was a thing much displeasing to Mr. Huxtable; but when I asked him the cause, he said he would tell me another time; which, indeed, he did, opening to me something of the high verity of love and its dark abuser, which dims the soul's bright eye. He said, that, as for the loose and promiscuous consorting with foreign women, commonly practised by seamen (which was the grounds of his displeasure at seeing those two at Pernambuc), it was of effect to distemper and corrode the healthful garment of the flesh like the moth of hell.

The merchant whom the Captain contracted with to supply our provisions, had agreed to have them conveyed to the landing-place an hour before sunset, being the hour that our men should make their return aboard the ship. Accordingly, having promenaded most of the town, and refreshed ourselves in an eating-house with some chocolate and Spanish preserves, very grateful and delicious, Mr. Huxtable told me, that, as he was willing to over-see the lading of the provisions, it was now time we took our way to the shore.

While we went, we saw, in one of the principal streets, a papist procession. As it passed all the church-bells began chiming with the solemn chanting of the choristers; and many large lean dogs rendered their responses (as it should seem) with a tumultuous loud barking.

"'Tis a brave sight," said I, when it was gone.

"So 'tis," said he dryly, "a brave sight indeed."

"Is it nothing but vain show?" said I. "I wonder, sir, if you consider of it so, as you seem to do by your accents, that you should put off your hat, as I saw you did, when it was passing by."

"No, truly," answered he, "it is not vain, in one way; for these people do set their trust in it—yea, put upon it a heavy load: not only their virtues and charitable works, but their sins, their cruel oppressive acts, their opprobrious vices: a heavy freight for such an airy craft; for 'tis but a ship of vanity, for all their confidence, and a superstitious fabric, for all its bravery and pomp."

While he spoke, we passed by a shop wherein were tame monkeys, parrots, parrakites, and other gaudy fowl; which gave me occasion to ask him (what I extremely desired) that he would buy me a parrot.

He kindly consented, and I soon possessed, in a handsome gilded cage, one of these prating birds adorned with pink and grey feathers.

It lifted its voice the moment we came out of the shop, and the words it uttered were *"Pax Vobiscum"* over and over, with a kind of guttural and affected benevolent tone; which set Mr. Huxtable a-laughing.

I asked him what it was. He answered that it was a sort of monkish salutation, "Certes," said he, "they have converted the very parrots!"

Our boats lay on a sandy beach near a steep hill; upon which there stood a house with a crane for lading or unlading goods (the arm, like the beam of scales, goes up and down with ropes, or pulleys, having hooks to take hold on the merchandise), which was an apparent mark to our direction.

When we arrived the place, most of our men were already come, and the boatswain stood impatiently blowing his whistle to hasten some of the others that we saw coming down the slope. Our provisions (being in crates) were already stowed—part in our long-boat, part in the jolly boat.

My parrot was an object of diversion to our men, who came gathering round to observe it; and "Well," said one of them—'twas one of those two that we saw consorting with the foreign women—"I wishes now as that I had bought one, at all hazards, I do."

"Well, why did not you?" said I.

"Well," said he, "I doubted the Captain had taken it amiss if I had brought a talking bird aboard our ship."

Leaving the others to follow after, Mr. Huxtable entered his boat, bidding me take my seat in the bows; which I did, having my parrot in his cage on my lap.

It uttered its monkish saying while they shoved off the boat; which seemed a fitting *Vale* for this gay and vociferous bird.

CHAPTER XII

Departure from Pernambuc

Early in the morning next day, the tide of flood being spent, we weighed anchor and went away, having a brisk land-breeze and fair weather.

When we were gotten out a good distance but still in sight of land, we went to the southward, as the wind (being now easterly) obliged us to do, and kept along by the shore; so sailing for five or six days; in which time nothing of moment did occur. The wind was very unsettled, between sea and land-breezes; but, at last, after blowing in short flurries for some days, it came to the southward; which was an occasion for us to stretch off to sea, on purpose to weather a great shoal which runs a great way out from the shore.

We sailed over this shoal, being seven or eight days after our departure from Pernambuc, at the deeper end (as was discovered by sounding). Whilst we were on it, our men—amongst whom, be sure, was Obadiah, none readier!—did take a great many fish, some being very strange, gaudy, outlandish creatures: the fishes in this part of the world appearing as numerous and as various as the fowls and the fruits.

Thereafter, we had some small westerly gales, squalls, and rain for four or five days (the wind faint and often shifting about, and lastly hanging in the south) being fallen between the verge of the south coasting Trade, and the south-east general or *true Trade*. In this time, we saw many dolphins about us, and some sharks, as well as shear-waters, being small black fowl that fly skimming the water; hence their appellation. We also saw a small whale, with its spout shining like a thin misty fountain.

The next day, the wind being easterly, we ran with it to the southward for some days; and now, besides shear-waters, many other birds came flocking about us. Some were near as big as geese, others as ducks; of which latter kind some were black, some grey, and some spotted black and white. These, called *pintado birds*, come sweeping along the sea in flocks, or else appear sitting afloat upon the water. They are foul-weather birds, and, accordingly, not welcome to seamen, especially if they come about a ship, as these did, presaging a storm.

The same night as we saw these ill-omened birds, the sun gilded the clouds very prettily, and then made them all glorious—those below pure gold, those above a very bright red, growing darker upwards—while it entered a smoky dark cloud that lay just above the horizon.

I admired the spectacle, standing with Mr. Huxtable beside the poop-railing; but he told me that he rather dreaded the consequences of it, and, that, especially considering the time of the year (being now winter), we should have a violent storm.

"And 'tis so also in the experience of our lives," added he, commenting, as his custom was, in philosophical mode; "for the soul hath her clouds and vapours no less apparent than the sky; whereon that internal sun shines with the like glowing and gaudy dark magnificence; and then you may expect its passionate and meridian storms. Provide for them in time, and hand your topsails; stand ready to take 'em in! as now our Captain will soon give charge to do. The world is full of signs, as well from within as from without—not one or two, but a whole conflux, if we have eyes."

I did not on every occasion—as now I did not—well understand the sense of his observations; yet I did always lay them up in my mind—yea, and in my book also!—having that respect and veneration towards my wise benefactor as not lightly to pass over his slightest word.

Now, what he feared concerning a storm duly happened to us; for the wind, blowing from the W.N.W., increased in the night; so that, upon going aloft in the morning, I saw we ran at a great rate before wind and sea, having no other sail but our main-topsails reefed and our fore-sail with the yard lowered about three-parts.

'Twas a wild and stormy seascape; a great tumbling, jostling sea; the heavens covered with rueful clouds; and sea-birds hovering above the waters, uttering their melancholy mews. A strange sight it was, from the poop, to see the petrels flocking close under our stern, whilst they slowly flew in our wake, patting the water, first with one foot, then the other—as I had read in Captain Dampier's *Voyages* that they do—and also how they got their name—in allusion to St. Peter's walking upon the Lake of Gennesareth.

This violent gale, lasting a day and a night, handsomely helped us on our course; though it was very uncomfortable to us when it rained, as it did often, pouring down from a black cloud as if the bottom was fallen out of some huge water-butt; and then it blew harder than ever; but, running so light before wind and sea, we shipped but little water. Afterward, when the weather abated, we went on to the eastward, with variable winds, and made, in general, very good runs.

CHAPTER XIII

Mr. Huxtable's Sorrow

Not to detain the reader too long at a time when nothing worthy remark did befall—at least, concerning the real scope of my narrative—I'll jump our succeeding course by relating no more than the briefest particulars.

Having, accordingly, made the Cape of Good Hope, and touched there to fill our water, we went on two days still to the eastward, and then steered away until we got in with the Trade wind. From thence, after seven or eight weeks going, with variable weather and much rain, and when we were in about the latitude of 20d. S., the wind suddenly began to blow excessive hard, and so continued, with brief intermission, about the space of two weeks; forcing us to run afore it, without any, or scarce any sail abroad.

At length it abated of its fierceness, and sank, leaving so faint a breath that our ship, which lay weltering in the swollen waves, was scarce able to steer. On the day following the skies cleared.

I saw Mr. Huxtable in grave discourse with the Captain at the break of the poop just before he took an observation of the sun with the quadrant; but indeed, he had appeared, of late, while the storm lasted, very heavy and anxious in his thoughts. Upon learning our position, he spoke something with an urgent low tone that I could not hear; nor the Captain's answer, only the close—"and this is on the very verge of the calms!"

"This will be a flat calm," said Mr. Huxtable—"and of how long continuance?"

He lifted up his hand, as he spoke, with a violent passionate gesture; and, immediately turning about, made his way down the ladder to enter the alley-way; the Captain standing looking after him, with a serious musing countenance, and a look in his eyes of compassion such as I had never supposed he had so much sensibility as to discover.

I did not see Mr. Huxtable again that morning until he came and sat him down to dinner; which he did with a heavy brooding mind, eating and speaking (if the Captain said anything to him) after a listless manner. I was grieved to see him so, and wondered what the cause was, and thence what design he had in going this voyage: which though I did in a manner conclude it to be something out of the ordinary, had not hitherto much engaged my thoughts.

Going on deck after dinner, we saw that a flat calm indeed was already setting in, with sultry hot weather: the wind, now in the last extremity, coming in faint breathings; the sun began to shine so hot it made the air like a glass-house.

The ship, under all her sail, lay slowly rolling, falling away, and coming to her course again, shaking her yards, and tolling of her bell until the evening. After the sun was set, however, the wind a little revived; which put us in better hopes.

That night I slept unquiet, dreaming and waking. At about the second or third time, lying with my senses more than ordinary keen in the moonlit cabin, that was brighter than day, I heard the sound of some commotion (as it should seem) in the forepart of our ship. I did take but little notice of this at the time, and it had quite passed away from my recollection, but for what befell after, as I shall relate.

I over-slept myself next morning by an hour and more; which upon observing (by a small clock, set up by the wall of my cabin), I wondered Mr. Huxtable had not sent, or come himself, to see for me: but, hearing, while I dressed myself, the sounds of hurrying to and fro in the 'tween-decks and of much stamping of feet aloft, I conceived that something more than ordinary was befallen to engage his thoughts.

For the rest, I was sensible, as well as by the sultry warmth of the air as by the ship's gentle motion, that we lay now quite becalmed: which, when I went aloft, as I did presently, was confirmed, and, indeed, lively apparent to me like a painted picture.

I beheld, against the dusky blue sky, the still, tall stacks of our sails, that hung drooping in the glare, and the blue-dark expanses of the sluggard ocean. What principally engaged my mind, however, was the spectacle of our men—even the whole ship's company—congregated under the quarter-deck, and the Captain standing, looking down upon them, with his hand gripping hold on the rail and a very angry countenance, being only restrained by Mr. Huxtable, who stood by his side, from a more violent behaviour.

As I stepped up behind them, the boatswain, standing a little advanced of the rest, was making a long speech; in which, at length, after much winding about, humble protestations, extravagant encomiums, and the like, he said abruptly:

"We wishes to enquire of Mr. Huxtable on a matter of apparitions and sea-devils: what should be thought on them, what evil they may work, and the like."

"Why, what a coil of nonsense is this!" cries the Captain. "Are you all gone stark staring mad?"

But Mr. Huxtable, with a "Sir, by your leave," stepped to the rail, and, smiling on the boatswain, "What can have prompted you, I wonder," said he, "to enquire on such a topic. I hope we have no hobgoblins aboard our ship."

"Well, your honour," answered the boatswain, "to be plain with you, we do be afeared of an apparition aboard, as was suspected afore by some on us, and was seen of my mate, Philip Campion, while he went about for to go below after his watch. He did see it plain in the bright moonlight, and it was terrible to see."

"Why, what was the appearance of it?" asked Mr. Huxtable. "But come! Campion," says he, turning short on the man (for he stood among them), "do you give me an account of this terrible apparition, where you did see it, and when, and what manner of shape it took: whether a horse, an ape, an ostrich, or plain Poor Poll!"

He spoke this with a satirical, yet pleasant hearty tone of voice. But Campion was diffident, standing mute with his head bowed, appearing all cramped and awkward, being an old, lean, large built man, having his arms and legs bended curiously awry; which gave him somewhat of a comical aspect, with his simple countenance, mild like a sheep's, and his straggling spare grey beard.

But, however, persuaded by the rest, and, indeed, jogged forth from their midst, he said presently, after a jolting halting manner:

"'Twas abaft of the round-house, your honour. 'Twas grim and terrible. It had great, green, staring, round eyes. Ay! ay! and a headpiece to him, rising up. Ay! ay! rising up like a peak of rock."

I am sure that my readers, remembering that horrid apparition I saw at the window of the mill and on two occasions after, will not marvel but that a chill damp came over me at this speech; so that I scarce restrained myself from uttering an exclamation.

"It rose up high and narrow," said Campion, continuing after a stop, "like to a rock dwindled at the top. It set me all over on a tremor to see his terrible grim pointed headpiece, rising up aloft of his terrible green gleaming eyes."

A murmur arose from the others upon this; but Mr. Huxtable, glancing shrewdly at me, immediately began to make them a speech, assuring them that he would consider of the matter, and admonishing them, that, even if it was an evil spirit that Campion saw, and not a mere creature of phantasy (which he thought much more probable), they had no cause to be afeared, but ought to repose their trust in God, who over all evil spirits exercised a controlling power.

And, while he spoke, that ancient, pious seaman, Giles Kedgley, standing a little apart from the rest, did sometimes interpose a confirmatory word, solemnly nodding his head; which weighted his words, and increased the contenting of their minds and the pacifying of their ghostly apprehensions.

But, whether or not a ghost did walk our ship, a dreadful imagination tormented me; which, when our men were dispersed, and the Captain (being very cross and sullen) had removed himself to the other side of the deck, I could not refrain myself from divulging to Mr. Huxtable; and, though he could not explain that affrighting correspondency of apparitions—I mean, the seaman's vision and mine—nevertheless the very act of confiding it to him, as well as the reasonable and robust expressions he used with me, sufficiently disburdened and fortified my mind. Thereupon, pleased, as he told me, with my wise forbearance in holding my tongue and not discovering anything to our men, he said that he would now content my curiosity by divulging to me his story and the occasion of our voyage.

But, understanding that I had not yet broken my fast, he went and made the steward provide me a meal, bidding me come to him afterward in his cabin.

He told me then, that, in a voyage to China, his wife and child going along with him, his ship was chased and taken by pirates, who would have murdered all aboard; but, obtaining speech with their Captain, he undertook, if he would spare them, to convey a rich ransom to him at a place that he should appoint; to which the pirate captain consented, but held his son for a hostage. He set him and his wife ashore on the India coast, allowing him a sum sufficient to defray their voyage to England. In the voyage his wife died, having been thrown into a languishing disorder by the encounter with the pirates and parting from her child.

Upon his sad coming home, being now only in hope to save his son, he learnt that the merchant-company in which the biggest part of his fortune was entrusted, had met with heavy losses; and, in order to raise the ransom, as well as the charges of the voyage to the rendezvous, he was obliged to sell his estate. The farmhouse was part thereof; and he continued to dwell therein by the kind allowance of the purchaser. Obadiah Moon was the pirate's emissary, sent to guide him to the rendezvous when he should be come into the India seas.

"I ever took Obadiah for a rogue," said I when he had ended. "But why did he send his letter by me, instead of bearing it himself?"

"That I can't tell you," said he, "unless it was a precaution, such hardy rogues being often exceeding timorous on land, where they are not in their element. But as to his chasing you, he told me (for I did ask him) that he desired a piece of service of you, but what it was he said he had forgot."

"Well," said I, "'twas a happy chance that I fell in with him, or I had never come to your door; and then I know not what I should have done, or what would have become of me."

"It is not everyone is beholden to a pirate," said he, smiling affectionately on me. "But never set your deliverance down to chance; like ungrateful men, that yet, if an evil thing befall them, are as ready, the other way, to accuse the providence of God. But who can tell what is evil and what is good? He sendeth good in evil guises; he useth all instruments, pirates no less than martyrs and saints. The hand that delivered you was the same as afflicted me."

He raised his eyes to those portraits of his wife and child that hung over against us by the wall and, in the illumination of a beam that shone obliquely through the porthole and fell full upon the picture of that beautiful lady, as it seemed to me, she smiled, looked graciously upon us from her golden frame; and I was sensible that her spirit was with us, and did bless us, supernaturally possessing (by what I can express) a larger space within and without the confines of the cabin.

The lovely countenance grew dim; or else my sight was misty with tears. I looked upon Mr. Huxtable, who sat gazing strange and rapt, and was enthrilled, on a sudden, by a sympathetic concordancy of wonder and joy that shined in his eyes. My soul was translated with a rapture such as cannot be uttered; enchanted as by the dazzling bright radiance of a celestial sun.

Of how long continuance was this extatical state—whether but a moment or much longer, I know not, since time seemed suspended. But there came—being at first, dull and vague, as a sound heard while you awaken from a dream in the night—a long loud knocking upon the cabin door.

'Twas one of our men, being sent by the Captain to acquaint Mr. Huxtable that there was sprung up a wind out of the S.E.

This was, indeed, welcome tidings; and, when he understood the sense—for he appeared not to hear at first, staring wide like one dazed—he rose up from his chair, and immediately went on deck; whither I followed him.

The new wind, though but faint, yet gave some hopes of delivering us from our prison of calms; and, holding pretty constant all day and most of the night, we made some leagues towards the N.E., thus a second time crossing the equator.

In the morning we had a flat calm, and sultry hot weather. Our ship was now gotten into a current, and lay driving slowly eastward.

CHAPTER XIV

Astonishing Mystery of the Pirate Ship

As we came out on deck, we saw some of our men standing together, looking earnestly out to sea on the larboard side. The weather was hazy, yet not so thick as it was when I came aloft after rising: and, looking that way, I presently espied, dim and phantom-like, the form of a large ship, having three masts.

In the same moment, Mr. Huxtable uttered an exclamation, gripping hold on the Captain's arm.

"A ship!" cried he, pointing with his finger. "Look! Do you spy it?"

"Ay," said the Captain, "I spy it. Go, bring me my glass," said he to me. "In my cabin. Haste ye!"

I went eagerly; for I did apprehend that this ship might be none other than that pirate vessel which Mr. Huxtable, as he told me, had adventured so far to seek.

When I returned, and gave the Captain his glass, instead of spying himself, he had the grace to present it to Mr. Huxtable; who took a long look; while the Captain and I stood mute and expectant observing him.

As he lowered the glass, I doubted he was disappointed of his hope, he did look so stern and pale.

"Is it the same?" asked the Captain.

"Yes, please God!" answered Mr. Huxtable, and immediately bid me go and fetch Obadiah, who was not anywhere to see on our deck.

I found him in the forecastle, lying along on his seaman's chest, asleep and snoring, with his mouth open. Indeed, he lay so sound, I had much ado to awaken him.

Being yet half asleep, he began to mutter, rolling of his blear eyes. But, perceiving me at last, he cursed and swore at me. Nay, I think he had done me a mischief; but I was beforehand in that, having drawn his teeth—I mean, taken his knife from him—before I awakened him.

But, however, having heard my errand, he rose up and went with me aloft to Mr. Huxtable; who, immediately giving him the glass, desired him to spy and tell him if he did know that ship.

The mist was now less, the ship appearing more plain; and Obadiah, having spied, answered:

"Ay! your honour, I do know't for sure. And who more than me should? asking of your pardon. We be fallen in with the old Captain; and I hopes he will regale me after my long travel. This be a very dry thirsty season, your worship; and, seeing as I have given you such a piece of news as must be hearty welcome to ye, I do make so bold as to ask if you will treat me," said he grinning.

But Mr. Huxtable only told him to be off; yet, as he began to move away, murmuring, he bid him stay beside the barricade.

Thereupon, turning to the Captain, he desired him to give charge to launch our ship's boat. "For I design," said he, "to go with this man, Moon, to yonder ship."

But this was too bold and impetuous a resolution to the Captain, who, lowering his glass (for he was spying), said vehemently:

"Sir, I hope you will do no such thing. To go with one sole man is but a rash and foolhardy adventure. I intreat that you will go, if go you will, in the long-boat. Give me leave, I will muster a crew."

"Nay, sir," said Mr. Huxtable, interrupting him. "I thank you for being so careful for me; but you know, don't you, that it was agreed with the pirate I should go alone—only with his emissary—this fellow, Moon; and the occasion is in no wise altered though we be fallen in with his ship at sea. 'Tis an unlucky chance, in one way, if he should take it into his head to molest us; for I am not willing to endanger our men, and did never think there would be occasion for it; neither will there be, I hope, in what I purpose. But let us make no delay in my going, lest, not knowing who we are, he should attack us in his boats, and, if they should come, and we could not make his men understand the business (which might well be, if he was not with them, because there might be no Englishman among them), we should be molested, and perhaps embroiled. If I do not return" (said he, with a lower tone), "you know what to do. Sir, I desire you will immediately give orders to launch the boat."

But the Captain began to object all manner of doubts and impediments, protesting that our men would willingly hazard their lives (which, no doubt, they would have done) to go with him; which put Mr. Huxtable quite out of patience.

"I cannot stand to parley with you," cried he, shortly interrupting him; "and if you do not immediately bid the boatswain lower our boat, I'll do so myself."

This stopped the Captain effectually. "Your servant, sir," said he, making a small stiff bow; and, stepping quickly to the rail with his face as red as fire, he called for Mr. Falconer in a sudden, furious loud voice. And, when he was come, having been on the forecastle talking with the carpenter, "What made you there?" cried he. "Do you esteem yourself one of the common seamen that you are so familiar with 'em? Belike you have a mind to mess with 'em in the forecastle."

Mr. Falconer returned some humble answer; which did enrage the Captain but the more.

"You appear to me," said he, with a bitter sarcastical tone, "to be liker a figure of earth, or of clay, than a reasonable man. Was you kneaded out of some Netherland flat? But let us see how you can move," said he, abridging his insulting speech as his eye fell upon Mr. Huxtable, who did look very angerly. "Have out the ship's boat. Haste ye, or I'll come down and give you a shog."

As he ended, Mr. Huxtable, scarce able to contain his indignation at this outrageous treatment of Mr. Falconer, betook himself abruptly to the gang-way; where Obadiah stood waiting while they launched the boat.

But when it was afloat, and Mr. Huxtable was setting his foot on the step of the ladder, such a pang of sorrow afflicted me, on a sudden, as I looked upon him, such a sharp apprehension of the danger he run in going to the pirate ship, such a searching desperate sense of desolation, that, if he had been my very father (as, indeed, he had treated me like the most affectionate of fathers), I am sure I could not have felt a sharper sense of it. Running forward, and catching hold of the skirt of his coat, I besought him, with tears in my eyes, not to go; or, at least, to let me go with him. When he told me that he could not, and was stepping into the boat, I desperately essayed to have followed him; but he turned and set me back to the gang-way, bidding me pluck up a spirit and not be so childish.

"And why should you be so fearful for me?" said he. "Come, you don't suppose, do you, that this pirate would put the treasure I bring in jeopardy for the sake of murdering me? What, do you think he would kill the golden goose?"

With this, he sat down; and, Obadiah entering after him, they took up the oars and pulled away through the small waves.

When they were gotten about a quarter of a mile, the Captain, who till then stood leaning with his arm on the gunnel, sometimes raising his glass to spy at the pirate ship, on a sudden turned away, and addressed himself, in somewhat of a mollified temper, to put the ship in a posture of defence, desiring Mr. Falconer to have small-arms (of which he had a store in his cabin) provided to our men, and the like. But our ship carried no guns, being in accordance with what the pirate captain had demanded.

While this was doing, comes to me the boatswain, taking the occasion when the Captain was gone below, and essayed to have gotten some intelligence from me, shrewdly suspecting that I knew something. But, however, having perceived his intent in time, I made a shift to fob him off by pretending to think the like of him, and to be willing to have drawn him. I believe he was seriously concerned for Mr. Huxtable, and the rest of them no less. Although they knew not the occasion, they divined he ran some hazard; and, when they were at leisure, they gathered together in knots of twos and threes to discourse, questioning among themselves in hushed low voices, solemnly wagging their heads.

In this manner the time passed, being about four hours (which was sufficiently long for me); until, a little after noon, to my great satisfaction, the ship's boat came in sight. Nevertheless, a weight came over me presently while I stood observing it; and, when it was gotten near and I could see Mr. Huxtable plain, I perceived things wrought not well, he did look so heavily, as if, indeed, he had been stunned.

When he was returned on board, I, stepping up behind him, heard him tell the Captain that the ship was, indeed, the pirate ship, but that it was quite deserted: not a soul on board; yet, notwithstanding, all her boats were aboard, and nothing, in any the least particular, seemed wanting or amiss. There was no appearance of any violence or disorder, either aloft or below; nor was there any lack, but plenty of provisions and of everything they wanted; and (to fill up the mystery) he found in the great cabin a chest full of treasure.

Mr. Huxtable and the Captain seriously debated this astonishing confounding enigma, while they paced, with slow steps, up and down on the deck. But, at dinner, which was presently served, they spoke but little, and ate but little too—Mr. Huxtable, looking dull and heavy as if he had suffered a blow (as, indeed, he had); the Captain, after passing his hand once and twice over his forehead, complained of a megrim; and, at last, with some muttered words of apology, he rose up from his chair and went and lay down on the settee in the stern.

Mr. Huxtable immediately after went out, and gave charge to Mr. Falconer to launch our jollyboat, designing to take another journey to the deserted ship.

When this was done and the crew was on board, I followed after him down the ladder, and (he not denying me this time) sat down beside him in the stern. He gave the order to pull away in a low dispirited voice; but the men, as if they were willing to signify their affection for him (for they did apprehend he suffered some sore disappointment), pulled lustily, toiling in the scorching rays of the sun; so that we soon approached the ship. But when we were gotten near, I began to grow afraid.

Void and solitary things, as deserted houses, and the like, do sometimes solemnly affect our thoughts; nor would my readers think me phantastical if I felt the same (and not the less since it was so mysterious) while beholding from our boat this great void ship, standing up still and silent, with her tall masts and heavy sagging sails that appeared of no ordinary bigness in the glassy air. Yet was there, in this my sense of it, more than emptiness, which could not of itself have daunted me. 'Twas a sense as of some horrid possession, as if a corpse should be possessed of a malign spirit casting his influence, thickening the sultry air. And this was mingled (I know not how) with some dreadful imaginations of what my grandfather had told me in his doctrine of hell; so that, in a horrid whimsey, I thought to see the deck suddenly burst asunder vomiting strange fire.

We spied a rope dangling down over the stern, which served us both to fasten our boat and to swarm up on board the ship. When we were all gotten aboard, Mr. Huxtable, bidding our men, and me also, to stay for him on the deck, immediately went below, taking Obadiah with him.

I began to rove about to see if I could spy anything extraordinary such as might explicate the riddle of the ship's being deserted. 'Twas a handsome ship—or rather, it had been so once; but much of the high, carved work had been shorn away, more than in our ship, and the gilt of what remained was much battered and the paint was peeled in the sun; the deck was covered with tar marks.

The open spaces were all of a shine; which made the shadows cast by the sails to appear the darker. The horror I conceived of the ship yet hanged upon my mind, and terrible outlandish phantasies came into my thoughts that it was enchanted—nay, that the crew had been spirited away, and that Mr. Huxtable and every one of us, while we stayed on board, was at any moment in danger of a supernatural power. What other cause (thought I) could possibly be conceived but something beyond natural for their leaving their ship, in all appearance, for no reason at all? I earnestly wished Mr. Huxtable's return, that, if anything should happen, I might be by his side.

But the glare was become fiercer this while; the heavens had a brazen appearance; the small waves moved sluggardly as in a sea of oil. I felt a drowsy torpor come over me; and, after taking two or three turns more about the deck, I went and lay down on a mattress that was spread near the main-mast. Whereupon, sinking into a sort of distempered sleep, I dreamt a dream, that was possessed with dark and inchoate images of horror.

I awoke, clutching the air in a transport; but, to my inexpressible content, beheld Mr. Huxtable standing by my side; and, stooping over me with a serious countenance, "Do not be afraid," said he, "'tis only a dream. Perhaps the sun has touched you, to make you dream so fearfully. I shall give you a draught from my medical-chest when we are returned to our ship."

"O, let us be gone immediately!" cried I.

"We shall soon be gone," answered he. "But I have not yet finished my search. Come! you shall return with me to the cabin, I'll show you a pirate's treasure."

I followed him to the great cabin; but, at the entry, he suddenly stopped, with his hand on the door-handle; and I, looking in at his side, stood perfectly astonished at what I did behold. For, on a high, carved, oak chair at the table, there sat a little plump man, having a smooth, sanguine, shaven countenance, dressed very neat in blue clothes, and wearing a peruke like our Captain's; and his present occupation was as strange as his being in that cabin, which Mr. Huxtable before had found empty; for 'twas nothing else but threading of little coloured glass beads such as children use to make necklaces. Neither, indeed, did he make the least stop in it now, nor showed any sign of being sensible of our coming. But, as I looked upon him, a sense of joy and efficacy came over me such as scattered away those vapours of horror from my mind.

"Who are you, sir?" asked Mr. Huxtable; but the little man returned no answer; nor appeared so much as to have heard him speak, but continued threading his beads.

"Why, what does he ail?" said Mr. Huxtable, stepping into the cabin. "Hi, sir! I do ask you who you are, and what your quality is aboard this ship."

"Well, this is a strange thing," said he, having still no answer; and, stepping to him, he laid hold on his arm. "Look you, sir," said he, "if you are pretending, or play-acting, for some design you have, I do assure you it will not do with me. Come! leave this child's game, if you please, and attend to me."

Upon this, the little man stirred in his chair, yet with never a look at us; and, rising to his feet, stepped slow and staid across the cabin, and opened a little door in the wall. He thrust his hand in, and took forth a book. This he set upon the table, being a manuscript quarto, covered with sailcloth. Hereupon, he returned, after the same astonishing odd manner, to his chair, falling again to his childish occupation.

The writing, which was in a small, neat character, was inscribed after the fashion of a journal-book. But this was all that I could see of it; for Mr. Huxtable was not willing that I should look it over. Neither would he tell me what it was; and what it signified he told me that he did not know.

"It's total amazement," said he, reading over the page, and turning others.

At length, he rose up, and made another endeavour to have spoke with our strange companion, inviting him to go with him to our ship.

"Why, this is the strangest thing of all!" said he, when nothing—neither speech nor sign—would serve, the little man continuing to thread his beads, smiling to himself as in a rapture. "You would think he was under some enchantment."

While he spoke, I was glancing my eyes round the cabin, which was extreme handsome, especially the walls being hung round with rich embroidered or painted cloths, with curved swords, or scimitars, daggers, and battleaxes, artfully disposed about brazen shields, several being richly overlaid upon the hilts with precious stones.

Over against the window in the stern, there stood a chest, bound with triple bands of iron. 'Twas unlocked; and I discovered within an ebony box, being not much smaller than the chest, very curiously wrought with the figures of elephants inclosed with forest trees. This was near full of jewels—as rings, set with diamonds, rubies, or emeralds, and the like costly trinkets—and of precious stones, some being in the crude or natural state. There were also five or six large moneybags as well as some pieces of plate, as silver tankards and a great goblet that looked to be of pure gold.

Mr. Huxtable, having already pried into this chest, told me he intended to take the ebony box with him to our ship. He lifted it out, and wrapped it over with a richly broidered cloth which he had taken down from the wall—unwilling, as I suppose, that it should be seen by covetous eyes. Thereupon, bearing it in one arm and the journal-book in the other, he once more addressed himself to that little man.

"Will you go with us," said he, "or do you desire that we shall leave you? I hope you will accept of our hospitality aboard our ship."

He returned no answer; but, after threading another of his beads, which he did very deliberately, he put the rest into his small box, set it in his coat-pocket, rose up, and followed us out, stepping slow and stiff in the manner of a somnambulist.

As we came out on the deck, our men looked surprised and perfectly dumbfounded to see who was with us, as well they might! But Mr. Huxtable immediately bid them go down into the boat; whither we followed them, with our burdens.

I took my place beside the little man, feeling wonderful happy, as before I did in the cabin. It was the hour of sunset; and my thoughts were raised up gay and splendid like the western glory.

CHAPTER XV

Mysterious Writing of the Little Mute Man and Discovery of a Monster

When we had recovered our ship, Mr. Huxtable took Obadiah apart from the rest, and asked him if he did know whether that little mute man belonged to the crew of the pirate ship; to which he answered vehemently that he had never set eyes on him in the whole course of his life.

Thereupon, Mr. Huxtable had the little man to the cabin; where the Captain awaited our return, reposing himself upon the couch. He rose up upon our entry, staring wide on our strange companion; who immediately went and sat him down on a chest that stood beside the wall, and pulled out his box of beads and his needle and thread. This quite amazed the Captain, who opened his mouth, as well as his eyes; but, not waiting for him to utter his astonishment, Mr. Huxtable briefly acquainted him with how the man was discovered in the cabin of the pirate ship, and what befell after, showing him the journal-book and the box, which he set open before him.

"That they should leave behind them such a rich treasure as this!" exclaimed the Captain, lifting his hands up, whilst he gazed on the jewels in a rapture. "But, come sir, let us see what is in this book, which, I hope, will make us a clearance; for, indeed (said he, in a gay smiling humour), it was put in your hands by one that seems as simple as a child."

"With all my heart, sir," answered Mr. Huxtable, with a dry tone, "and certainly 'tis clearly writ."

Hereupon, we all removed to the table; whereon Mr. Huxtable set the journal-book open at a page. This was written in a small distinct, though somewhat unsteady hand. He began to read as follows:

My senses begin to swoon as when I beh (these last three words and the beginning of the fourth—I mean, *beh*—were struck through). *Either I shall perish or else lose my wits, and, therefore would leave some record. 'Twas soon after dark, when, as I sat in a muse after study, I became sensible of something unwonted. A green light shined through the walls of the cabin. I hasted up...*

"And there you see," said he, "'tis broke off. There's nothing after; and the foregoing entries (for I have looked them over) are merely natural observations, as of plants, beasts, and the like, that, as I suppose, he saw in some places he visited. Nay, I had forgot; there is one I intended to look at again, which is concerning a *sea-savage*, that seemed to me somewhat remarkable. But, however, we won't stay for it now, but examine into what is here; for 'tis sufficiently strange. What can the meaning be? What possibly can have happened to this man, whether or no he is the same as him we have with us," said he, glancing over his shoulder at that strange mute, who continued to thread his beads.

"Ay, and what was become of the rest?" said the Captain. "Why was he the sole man left on the ship? Sure, they were all cast into the sea by pirates; for, if they had meant to transport them into slavery, they would have conveyed them in their own ship."

"But they were pirates themselves," said Mr. Huxtable, "You don't suppose, do you? that if they had been assaulted by other pirates, they would have yielded without firing off a gun; for, you know, there was no appearance of any violence on the ship."

This put the Captain to a stop; and, while he sat puzzling in his mind, I could not but wonder how Mr. Huxtable could expect any light from such a beclouded sphere. But perhaps he only designed to use him in the manner of a flint stone to strike out the sparks of his own cogitations.

But suddenly the Captain started off anew. "Why, I have it!" cried he. "'Tis plain as daylight. They spy a ship, chase her and take her without firing off a gun, while this naturalist is sunk deep in his studies; find her to be a rich prize—or, at any rate, very convenient for them—a better ship to cruise in than what they had. So all remove into her, having cast her crew into the sea, and so away, either forgetting their precious naturalist, or, more likely, glad to be rid of such philosophical gear. He, breaking off his studious meditations, and finding himself alone and forsaken on the ship, goes stark dancing—or, as I should rather say—*silent mad*, and conceives a peck of moon-stuff about a green light, and the rest, which, being to the manner accustomed (I mean, one of these scribblers), he writes out and describes, until he falls into some mad fit of silence, as he continues in to this hour."

He ended with triumphant accents, and I must confess it did seem remarkable to me. I now looked with more respect upon the Captain, thinking that the great puzzle was now quite cleared, and expecting Mr. Huxtable would be in the same opinion. But his countenance did not change, and he said:

"Sir, it's possible you are in the right, and I cannot myself render a better explanation. But I am much in doubt, nevertheless, and rather think there is some deep mystery in it not to be resolved by taking this writing for the vapourings of a madman, which it does not appear to be; and you seem to have forgot the treasure. Though they should forget or abandon their naturalist, you can scarce conclude they would do the like of a rich treasure."

This was a shrewd discouragement to the Captain, who looked very foolish. But, soon recollecting himself, "Sir, I see not," said he, "that the treasure is such a great impediment as you suppose. First, how do you certainly know it might not belong to this naturalist? And then, as I have heard such rogues do commonly keep faith with each other, they would not have robbed him, but left it with him in the ship. Sir, I think my reasons hold; and you own you can't think of better."

"Pirates, abandoning a ship, do not commonly leave her swimming," replied Mr. Huxtable. "But I would beg of you to consider this entry more particularly, which I deny not is sufficiently odd, but connected, not mad gibberish.

"*My senses swoon again*" (said he, passing his finger under the words), "and, you see, he added and afterwards blotted *as when I beheld*, the last word being but half writ. Why did he blot it? Very like it run impetuous off his pen from his disordered thoughts, set, on a sudden in a ferment, and he intended to have deferred it until he came to relate what befell, or what he saw, after he *hasted up* (as he says), but from some cause was prevented; for that is the place, you see, where the entry is broke off. 'Tis coherent from beginning to end; and this natural stop in the order seems the more to aver it."

The Captain was going to interpose at this juncture; but, without giving him the time, and as if he spoke rather to himself than to anybody else, Mr. Huxtable went on:

"And what can be thought of the *light*? It was a *green light* he says. It *shined through the walls of the cabin*. How could a light, whether green or white, or any other colour, shine through wooden walls? Does he mean only through the port? But why, then, does he write *through the walls*? Sure, such a naturalist had been more exact. Well, I shall not absolutely deny—"

He broke off, and we all three started round in our chairs; for the little mute man, whom by this time we had almost forgot, was risen up from his place, and stepped, with slow steady gait, to the table.

He reached forth his hand to the journal-book; and, having turned a page, stooped over in a posture as if he would write. When he had so continued for a while, with his arms on the table, his hand begun to move over the page.

Hereupon, Mr. Huxtable quickly provided him with a pen, setting it in his hand; and, as it did rest too loose and unsteady, he contrived to stay it with his finger and thumb, but, so as not to hinder the motion. Thereupon, it begun to write, although but as the insignificant scribble of a child, running on in an unhandy scrawl. But, after a while (Mr. Huxtable dexterously replenishing the ink), we begun to perceive characters, and then words and phrases in it, as *glass blue cinnamon*, which was repeated in the next line, followed by what looked to be *sunflower*, and, two or three lines further, *rock pillar*.

Hereupon it fell away into mere scribble, and presently ceased.

We waited to see if he would continue; but he never did; and, after sitting awhile in the same posture, he rose slowly up from the table, and stood still, with that look in his eyes like a little happy child that is dreaming.

Mr. Huxtable pulled the journal-book towards him, and begun to study the writing, the Captain and I stretching our necks at either side of him to see.

"This is in the very latitude of limbo," said the Captain at last. "Sir, you have conveyed an antic aboard our ship."

"It should seem so, I do own," answered Mr. Huxtable; "but it's possible this man is in some rapt state beyond his ordinary senses, and, as in dreams there commonly appear some images or phantastical representations of things fallen out in our daily lives: so, as I conceive, what he hath writ so strangely, and (as it should seem) so foolishly, may be in a state comparable with dreams, wherein perhaps he hath intermingled something of actual experience. Such may be those words, *rock pillar*, which appear to signify something to the matter, though sufficiently puzzling. And *Summer House, cinnamon and blue*—"

He ceased, murmuring over the words, with a look in his eyes as if he was fallen upon some wonderful pleasant thoughts.

The Captain also was silent; though once and twice I observed him to open his mouth as if he would have spoken. 'Twas as if he was hushed by some spell.

Suddenly starting up from his chair, he began to rove about the cabin, with his hands clasped behind him; and "Well, sir," said he after an extravagant affected manner, mincing his words; "I do humbly yield to your opinion and judgment in this matter; for it's Latin and Greek and Hebrew to me. Not that I am altogether unlearned in the Latin tongue. I do recall now being asked by my worshipful friend, Mr. Daniel Walderville, of Walderville Park and Manor in the county of Northumberland, whose ancestor, you know, was endowed with that ilk by William the Conqueror. I recollect, I say, that he did desire me, on a day, to explicate his coat of arms—I mean, the *motto*, of which he had forgot the signification.

"*I know you are more of a scholar than I am, says he; and it puts me out to be stumbled with it, as I was this day by Mistress Margaret* (that was Sir John Oldford's daughter). *Plague on it, and them that invented such foolishness!* cries he, being, like many of that degree—I mean, of ancient lineage—somewhat of a choleric complexion. *May the foul fiend take it and them also!* says he, and dings it from him across the room—I mean, a silver plate that he held in his hand, bearing this motto.

"*Tell me what it is,* says he. *Nay, set it down fairly in writing for me, and I shall put it in my bosom to have it in readiness.* And so he did when I had writ it out for him, and was no more troubled with it after. But I do ask your pardon: for I have been carried off my course."

"I don't deny, sir, but that you are gotten a point or two away from it," said Mr. Huxtable pleasantly; and, looking upon him, I perceived some happy delightful change was come over him. As for me, I was sensible, and had been almost from our entry into the cabin, of such enchanted glad spirits as I had known on the former occasions when I was in the presence of the little mute man.

"Certes, it's a prodigious puzzle," said the Captain, seeming to collect his vagrant thoughts. "What in the world has become of 'em? And there's this writing. All moon-stuff! Damme! I have it! They were all run dancing mad, like this one, and cast themselves into the sea, belike for thirst. But no, that won't do; for you did say you found plenty of water aboard. What can a man think? Sir, I shall beat my brains no more with it, by your leave. We do but lose our time with considering into it, and work ourselves into the latitude of limbo."

He had scarce ended when there came sounds as of footsteps in the alley-way; yet, nevertheless very unlike ordinary footsteps, being heavy and shambling soft as the foot-pads of some large animal.

This was an odd queer sound to hear in our ship; it enthrilled me with an obscure fear. But when presently the door of the cabin was set violently open, my heart-beats seemed to stop; for there appeared a figure of monstrous fashion. 'Twas squat and shaggy dark, having prodigious great limbs and hands and feet, that were webbed as a fish's fins, or a manatee's flappers; but his face, with its dwindled high peaked forehead, and great globular black glistering eyes, was like to that dreadful apparition I vaguely beheld three several times before, in manner related and described.

'Twas but for a moment; for the monster immediately turned and betook himself away. Mr. Huxtable was risen to his feet; and he and the Captain stood staring very wild. In the next moment, they made a rush to the door, myself following, and so forth, through the alley-way, to the deck.

There we saw our men running together and crying aloud, being almost beside themselves with amazement and terror. The boatswain, stepping to us, pointed with his finger, that did shake as with the fit of an ague, towards the starboard side. "There it went," cried he. "There it vanished away. Mercy on us, the dreadful sea-devil!"

We hasted to the place, but saw nothing save the small calm waves; although there was moonlight enough for discovery if the monstrous creature had been anywhere to see swimming in the water.

"Are you sure you did see it enter the sea?" said Mr. Huxtable to the boatswain, who, with the rest, was crept up behind us.

"Ay, your honour," said he; "I saw him leap up and overboard, and did hear the plash he made in the water; and these saw and heard also, most on 'em—didn't ye, messmates?"

"Ay," added he, when, with nods and vehement acclamations, they answered him, "there's no manner of doubt on't. He be returned to the sea, whence he came. I have heard tell of these sea-devils, but did never believe in 'em before. Howsoever, as he do appear to be in the course of nature—I mean, as having body and bones, and not one of these unearthly grim ghosts—I see not why we should be much in dread of him, though he be a proper monster, that's true. But as for me, I cares no more for him now than if he was some manner of sea-beast, or savage creature (as, I suppose, he is, if you consider of it), or *merman*, as your honour might call him."

Mr. Huxtable nodded in assent to this; and thereupon, one of the others laughing aloud, he enquired what diverted him.

"Why, master," answered he (being the carpenter's mate, a brisk merry fellow), "I was a thinking that if the mermaids be no more comely than this-here merman is handsome, we shall be the less endangered of our hearts and eyes."

This made the others laugh also, and provoked some more sallies of such uncouth wit; which Mr. Huxtable, as I observed, was rather glad of, as tending to put our men in the better humour; yet, careful lest the Captain, who stood muttering to himself, should fly out in a passion at this indecorous conduct, he immediately dismissed them.

CHAPTER XVI

Obadiah's Narrative

"Well," said the Captain, recovering his tongue, while our men dispersed, "this is nothing else, as I suppose, but what those fools took for a ghost in the ship, the monster lying somewhere concealed, or else, perhaps, going and coming; but who could have thought that there could be in all the world such a horrible hobgoblin?"

"No doubt but it is the same," answered Mr. Huxtable; "but Will here will have it that he saw this extraordinary strange creature before we embarked"; and briefly related those several apparitions.

"But now," said he pleasantly, turning to me, "I hope, like the boatswain, you will be the less affrighted. The hobgoblin, more substantial than such terrors use to be, has made his congee, and taken, I doubt not, a lasting farewell. He will scarce expect further entertainment amongst us."

"But there's a matter," added he, returning to the Captain, "which may not be irrelevant to this sea-monster, and that's what, I doubt not, you have remarked no less than I have—the prodigious eagerness Obadiah Moon has been in to get supplies of fish; but perhaps you may think this too extravagant a notion."

"Nay, sir," answered the Captain, swaying his body from side to side in the last degree of exasperation, "I shall not henceforth think anything too extravagant; for, I protest, I am gotten into such perplexity and downright amazement, I am not in a condition to deny anything. If devils can embark, if monsters and infernal furies can come on board our ships, they may feed on milk and pap, for me! And dazzling lights may shine through cabin walls, and Bedlamites may scribble enchanted revelations—sir, you shall have it as you will; I'll give o'er, and swallow anything. But this rogue, Moon," said he (becoming calmer), "hath he a hand in it, think you? Why, how can that be?"

"I do not absolutely affirm it," replied Mr. Huxtable; "but I think it looks very strangely"; and thereupon proceeded to run over the several occasions which Obadiah had employed to provide himself with supplies of fish with such liberality; which discovered to me that he had observed more than I thought.

"Well, sir," said the Captain, "let us immediately have him into the cabin to examine into it. If it is as you suspect, and he has had this monstrous creature concealed aboard the ship—I suppose, in the hold—but who could have thought? 'Fore George, sir, 'tis incredible! But, if 'tis so, I shall recompense his Moonship, I'll warrant him, with something of a sharper relish than salt fish!"

"Certainly we shall examine into it," answered Mr. Huxtable; "but first let us ask Mr. Falconer if he saw the creature. I wonder he did not come to us."

"Yes, why did he not?" cried the Captain, starting round. "I'll be a *falconer* to him; I'll—Hey! come you hither, Mr. Falconer," he bawled out, while he took a step towards the quarter-deck.

But Mr. Falconer, standing in his station as if nothing beyond ordinary had happened, neither answered nor made the least change in his posture—no, not after the Captain called a second time; which enlarged his choler to that degree, he ran down the deck, with his fists clenched, crying:

"Stock as a fish, the cold-blooded swab! Will nothing move ye? Must the heavens fall?"

Our men stood watching this violent transport of the Captain; while Mr. Huxtable started off after him. "What do you mean?" said he. "Is this a time to vent your childish spleen, with our men so overwrought?" which vehement expostulation availed.

But Mr. Falconer continued to stand beside the bulwarks in a posture remarkably rigid, bringing to my remembrance how I saw him that night of the ghost-scare among our men; and, as on that occasion, so now, he looked of a deathly pallor in the moon. As we approached near to him, however, he swiftly turned his head as if he beheld some strange thing in the air, his eyeballs, that appeared vacant and glazed, seeming to gleam with a sort of veiled feverish light.

The first to speak to him was Mr. Huxtable.

"Why, what do you ail, Mr. Falconer?" asked he. "You don't seem to be yourself. The Captain has twice called you."

"But 'tis to no purpose," said he, breaking off. "He is in some strange state, and cannot hear a word."

"Strange state!" exclaimed the Captain, smiting his breast. "Sir, I hope now you will give me leave to wonder if—"

He stopped, staring on Mr. Falconer, who, after once more swiftly turning his head from side to side, begun to mutter wandering disjoined words, signifying, as well by the tone as the look in his eyes, some powerful wild amazement.

For a while he was silent, and then started off anew; but now, indeed, he seemed to be in the toils of some fearful dream, starting forward with his face all writhed up, so that it was a dreadful thing to see, while he uttered panic words concerning (as it should seem) a frightful idol.

Soon, however, he fell silent, and ceased to look so wildly, while his eyes closed. Fetching a sigh, he opened them again, and looked hazily upon us, passing his hand across his brow like a man awakening out of sleep.

Mr. Huxtable would have spoken to him; but, on a sudden, there arose such an alarum and commotion among our men as made us quickly turn about. They were all run together on the larboard side; and, looking where two or three pointed with their fingers, we beheld, at about a cable's length from our ship, something moving in the water, which, by all appearance, was nothing else than that savage strange hideous creature that had leapt into the sea.

The Captain, the moment he did spy it, bade me haste and bring him his pistol, which hanged on a pin in his cabin, reproaching himself, with an oath, for not having provided himself already.

When I returned, the head was no longer to see, and most of our men stood narrowly watching for it. But, over against the hatch, the carpenter's mate stood in a dispute with Obadiah Moon, who was just come aloft, being heavy and sullen with the effects of his drunken drench; and some wild expressions that he uttered startled me, bringing me to a standstill. "Be he the Captain, or be he the King himself," cried he, "if he do murder Jerry, I'll murder him!"

This diverted the other exceedingly. "Why, *Jerry*," said he, clapping his hands to his sides, yet with a vigilant eye for Obadiah's drawn knife. "Ho! ho! ho!—*Jerry* is good. A brave handsome *Jerry* he be, I warrants you! Say, messmates," cried he, bawling out to two or three of the rest who stood looking round on them, "would you know the hobgoblin's name? This-here mooncalf can tell 'e—"

But, being afraid to keep the Captain waiting, I had already started off, so that I heard no more. However, I resolved to acquaint Mr. Huxtable with what Obadiah had said; since his speaking of that monstrous creature so familiarly, seemed not a little to confirm his suspicions. Him I found in a dispute with the Captain, the occasion being the Captain's intent to shoot at that monstrous creature; which Mr. Huxtable did not desire, but only if it should attempt to come on board to offer us any violence.

On my stepping to him with his pistol, therefore, he received me after a furious manner, snatching it out of my hand and railing at me for having been gone so long upon his errand. Thereupon, as if he was ashamed of this violent behaviour, he removed himself to the further side of the deck.

Mr. Huxtable, meanwhile, was assisting the mate, who was recovered his senses but looked very shaken and infirm, to his cabin; which disappointed my desire to acquaint him about Obadiah.

That wretched creature, being by this time sufficiently sober (as it should seem), was parted from the carpenter's mate and the rest that made sport of him, and his present occupation was remarkable as tending to confirm those suspicions yet the more; for he kept roving along up and down the ship, with his eyes searching the sea all about, sometimes glancing round, as I suppose, to see if he was observed. But no one took any notice of him, unless by way of jest; only the boatswain, standing near the main-mast smoking tobacco, did sometimes observe him with a shrewd meditative eye. After a while, however, yielding his vain searching, he betook himself below into the forecastle.

He was scarce gone when Mr. Huxtable returned aloft, and mounted to the quarter-deck. Thereupon, after looking up and down, he called to know where Obadiah was; and, when I told him, he sent me to bid him immediately to present himself in the cabin.

"If you will go with me," said he to the Captain as I set off, "we shall presently interrogate this fellow whether he can tell us anything."

I found Obadiah laid sprawled along upon his seaman's chest, with a bottle of rum in his hand, which he dangled after the manner of a babe. This childish tender appearance was immediately belied, however, by the surly and lowering look that came into his eyes, and (as I may say) eclipsed the foolish moon of his countenance, as soon as he beheld me, concluding, perhaps, or else suspecting, on what errand I was come.

"What do 'e want aboard of me?" cried he, when I had told him Mr. Huxtable's bidding. "Can't he leave a poor seaman in peace? I have a head on me like as it might be fashioned out of cork. Do 'e go and bear word I be too sick to go. Do 'e now," said he with a whining tone, "and I'll give ye a cur'osity. I have brave cur'osities such as you have never seen the like, I promise you; and I'll show them to you, and you shall have the one as likes you best, if so be as you will bear word to Mr. Huxtable saying and showing of him that I be very sick. I do think verily," said he, setting his hand to his brow, "that I have taken a mortal bad distemper and be very sick."

"I shall do no such thing," said I, returning smartly on him. "What you ail is drinking too much rum. You had best go with me and make no more delay; for by this time Mr. Huxtable and the Captain will be waiting for you."

"What! the Captain too," cried he, and uttered a horrible curse, while he begun knocking his head with his fist as if he would scatter away the drench of his potations. But, however, he rose up and followed me, murmuring all the while until we were come to the cabin.

At our entry, Mr. Huxtable, looking on Obadiah with a stern aspect, signed to him with his finger to stand before him; which was much unpleasant to Obadiah, for, being over against the stern-window, he stood blinking in the moonlight with his blear-eyes.

"What may it be as your honour wants along of me?" said the miserable creature, Mr. Huxtable's gaze being worse to him, I doubt not, for the shine. "I have a head on me like as it might be dead wood, with a turning in my innards like, as you might say, a wind-vane, it do turn and turn so dizzy."

"Well, it's no wonder if you have, sirrah!" answered Mr. Huxtable smartly. "You know, I suppose, the name of that."

"I would not go for to give a name to't, your worship," said Obadiah surlily, "unless I might call it by a name as would be an affront to the ears of gentlemen such as you are."

"Rum," said Mr. Huxtable, "is the name of it. But that's beside the business we have in hand; and, if you can't stand easy on your legs, you may draw a chair up and sit."

The Captain was going to exclaim at this, but held his peace upon a look from Mr. Huxtable; and, saying "Thank'e, your honour, thank'e kindly," Obadiah went and drew one of the chairs along before the settee.

"I suppose, Mr. Moon," said Mr. Huxtable after a dry sarcastical manner, when Obadiah was sat down, "that to be forsaken by your familiar friend, your beloved mate, after so dear a bond of amity, must be extreme afflicting to you. Can you think of any cause why he should part company with you so sudden? Did you fall out in any point, *as for instance, in regard to supplies of fish?*"

This set Obadiah all on a heap; and he sat staring on Mr. Huxtable with a foolish face; but the Captain gave him a shog.

"Come! come!" said he with a high angry tone. "Will you sit like a log, or dummy? Did you not hear what was said to you? What have you to answer? Heh?"

Upon this, the uncouth malcontent heaved himself up in his chair, and said with a whining and dismal tone:

"What you ha' been asking of me be all dark to me, your worship. I ha'nt no partic'ler mate as I knows on, except my mate, Ephraim Sawkins; but we an't so partic'ler close and familiar in consorting but what we might be more, d'ye see? (begging of your honour's pardon). Nor he an't parted company with me no more than what he is commonly not so close, as I was a saying of, but only, in a manner of speaking, *fo'c'sle mates*, as you might say. And what you say about supplies of fish, I knows nought on't. It's true, your worship, as I have a partic'ler relish for it, but that be no—"

"Enough!" cried Mr. Huxtable, abridging him. "In vain you endeavour to fob me off with your foolish prevarications. You know very well what my meaning is—what companion, or mate, you had with you; how you hid him in the ship and fed him on fish. Confess and make a clean breast, you had better! For, if you do, and leave nothing out, and tell me how and when you did come by this outlandish companion, and why you brought him with you on the ship, and anything else appertaining, we are minded to deal leniently with you; but if not—"

At this juncture, he was obliged to break off to speak to the Captain, who plainly signified his displeasure at such mildness. When he had pacified him, he continued, with a weighty and grave tone, assuring Obadiah that he intended to deal as hard with him if he dissembled, as he would be mild and forbearing if he should discover all, and warned him to beware how he answered, lest he should run himself on a needless severity and punishment. He ended frowning; while the Captain looked surly on.

Obadiah for a space answered nothing, only swayed himself from side to side in his chair, as if in the measure of his uneasy thoughts. At last, he delivered himself as follows: for I do remember the rude, rambling manner of it very well:

"Why, your worship" (said he), "you, and my duty also, admonishes me to unlade all before you, leaving nothing out, concerning this-here matter what you have inquired of me; for I do confess as I demeaned myself as I ought not, albeit intending no harm, and like as if a seaman should buy a parrot, or an ape, and take it aboard ship with him, as this young gentleman did when we went ashore at Pernambuc. Not as I denies but that there be summat more to't than that is.

"And, having regard as it is a matter which so nearly concerns you and what you're after in this-here voyage, I makes bold (bating not your worship's promising to pardon me, which I am deeply sensible of, and render thanks with a full tide)—I makes so bold as to beg of you a little more. I am, as your worship doth know, but an humble poor seaman, having little in this world but what I do bear about with me, in my belt, or in an old cotton cloth; and seeing as it be come into my thoughts after hearkening to your worship's gracious admonishing discourses to us seamen on the deck—it be come into my thoughts—"

"Bless us!" cried the Captain at this juncture, breaking in, "will you never come to your course? Will you not? Heh?"

But Mr. Huxtable, with a stern tone, bade Obadiah to proceed; and he continued after a halting manner.

"I was a-saying, your worship" (said he), "being emboldened and drawn on by your worship's kindness, as that, when I was ashore once more in my native country, I took up a resolution to leave following the sea, which has been my ruin and undoing all my days; for it be crabbed and lean—the sea, your honour—villainous lean to the soul. So, as you was so kind in what you says to me, it was come into my thoughts you would give me some hopes to lead a better life and repent me of my sins when I be come ashore again in my native country (as, please God, we all shall!); seeing, I mean, as what I can tell you is of such concernment to ye, and so powerfully aiding the intent you have in this-here voyage. And it is but a matter of a few pounds as I am asking of, for to buy a snug small cottage with a garden to it, and—"

"And an orchard, may be, and a grove of pear trees," said Mr. Huxtable satirically, abridging this impudent request. "Nay, I had forgot to add a fish-pond; else, where would you provide your supplies of fish? For, I suppose, you don't intend to banish your precious companion and dear beloved crony from your cottage paradise. You have one virtue, Master Moon, you are not tardy in seeking; and I wish I could think you was honest in your rural hopes. But there's no end to your cheats and impudence; and if you do not immediately proceed with your relation, and if I should perceive anything false or equivocating (for I am no seagull—or I should say, rather, I am no *fish* to be took with your bait), I do assure you, I shall have you set down on the ballast and not illiberally provided with chains."

This severe admonishment was enough for Obadiah, who appeared to bow beneath its burden; and he did continue in sober earnest.

"Well, your worship," said he, "this-here, what I shall be telling you, is what fell out plain and faithful, and not leaving anything out, begging of your pardon for the liberty I run into, a hoisting up too much sail, in a manner of speaking.

"I was aboard of a ship of you know who; but whether the Captain knows (begging your worship's pardon) I knows not."

"Ay, ay," answered Mr. Huxtable, "the Captain is acquainted with my business with your Captain. You need not make any stop or concealment, but plainly tell all out."

"Thank'e, your worship," said Obadiah. "Well, then, as I was a-telling you, I was aboard of our ship what was cruising in these seas, and, as I recollect, not far from where we now lies. It was not above a year ago, as I particularly remember, it being my natal day, which I always keeps and celebrates."

"By drinking, belike," said the Captain sarcastically.

"I do not deny it, your worship," replied Obadiah, "for there an't no harm, as I says to myself, in drinking down a dram for to celebrate my natal day."

"The more by token because nobody else will celebrate it, I suppose," returned the Captain.

"On! on!" cried Mr. Huxtable, with a furious impatient tone, which silenced the Captain sufficiently. "About a year ago, you say, you were cruising in these seas—well?"

"Ay, your worship," answered Obadiah, "and we had such calm and sultry weather as we have at this present; and the first thing I spied, when as I looked out in the morning, was what your worship is pleased to call my *companion*, what was a-swimming in the sea close under our larboard bow. At first, I took him for some wild Indian; but when he come about in the water and I saw him plain, it did set me all on a tremor. For I beheld him the first time, and was not yet grown accustomed to him, as after I was. For we did entice him on board our ship and made much of him. But, if it had been in the moonlight when I first beheld him, and not sunshine, as it was, the stark grim sight of him had set me beside my wits."

"You enticed him on board your ship?" said Mr. Huxtable. "How did you contrive to do it? He did not come readily—did he? But

I have yet to hear what this extraordinary strange savage creature may be."

"Ay, ay, he did come ready, your worship," answered Obadiah. "You might suppose as that he was come a purpose, or sent, he did come so ready. He was a-swimming close aboard. I hallooed, and the rest of our men come crowded to the side, though much afeared when they catched sight of his figurehead.

"Some were for letting fly at him with their pistols; but our quartermaster stopped that, and sent one to call the Captain, that lay abed (for he was ever a late riser). But while this was doing, it had quite amazed ye, as it did me and all of us—and terribly frighted us, too—to see him rear himself up out of the sea, and come clawing up the side with his fish-claw hands, and his blubber head, and his terrible grim visage. We thought we should all be murdered to death; and we run scattering all about the deck, some swarming up the ratlines. Trust me not if we did not think it was a devil come up out of the sea to murder us all and deliver up our souls to the Evil One, like as it might be a catch of fish; for the Evil One doth ever use to keep his fish-hooks and nets overboard, in a manner of speaking, for to take and catch up poor mariners."

CHAPTER XVII

Obadiah's Narrative Continued

At this juncture, Obadiah, who was become much more easy and free in his relation, made a stop; and, after observing Mr. Huxtable awhile with his crafty small eyes, said after a slow halting manner:

"I be willing to go on and furnish you, your worship, in every part, concerning what I be now come to tell you, how I came to consort with what you calls my *companion*, as well as what did after befall; but, being little accustomed to the manner of speaking long on end, my mouth and throat is all parched" (said he, writhing his lips), "like sand for dryness. If your worship would but give me a dram to drink, I should make the better way."

Upon this, Mr. Huxtable bade me provide him a drink of water; which was not the sort of dram that he wanted. But, however, *making a virtue of necessity* (as the saying is), he took and drunk it down, looking round afterward with somewhat of a sour countenance.

"See that you make no more stops," said Mr. Huxtable, while Obadiah returned the cup into my hand, "or I shall quite take back and cancel the pardon I offered you. Go on, sirrah, and do not palter!"

This memento sufficiently brought Obadiah to his course; and, having excused himself after an obsequious manner, "I was relating, your worship," said he, "how that *Jerry* (as I afterward called him) came aboard our ship. We had no cause to be so scared of him; for he never offered anybody the least violence, and was as harmless as a turtle-dove. We made much of him, and gave him pork and biscuit; but he never would go for to eat nothing else but fish, which he ate very hearty; which was the occasion I wanted so much fish for to feed him.

"He was very diverting to all on us as soon as we was become accustomed to him; and our chirurgeon, Mr. Vertembrex, was much taken with him, being, as you might say (begging your worships' pardon) a sort of cur'osity, or outlandish discovery, such as Mr. Vertembrex much affected, and would write of 'em in his journal-book—"

"Hold," cried Mr. Huxtable, interrupting him. "What was this Mr. Vertembrex? Not the same as him I found in the abandoned ship?"

"Ay," replied Obadiah, "he was the same, your worship, and no other."

"Why, you plainly told me," said Mr. Huxtable, "that he was not with you on your ship, and that you had never seen him before!"

"I did much amiss, your worship," answered Obadiah, with a whining tone, "and I do own and confess it, and asks your pardon."

"But what reason could you have for lying to me?" asked Mr. Huxtable. "What possibly could it profit you to deceive me in such a point as this?"

"No profit at all, your worship," said he. "But I was afeared you would get the wind of my having Jerry lying concealed in the ship. It don't signify of itself, that's true; but, *as all rivers flow into the sea* (as the saying is), how could I be certain sure but what, if you should have got the wind in one quarter, it might not waft ye to the other? I did much amiss, as I owns and confesses, but now makes amends by a-telling of you plain and faithful; and so I hopes as you will pardon me and suffer it to drive astern."

"You're a great rogue," said Mr. Huxtable; "but, as you have confessed, and I find you in other points honest in your relation, I'll pass it over. Continue where you broke off, which was of the creature you call *Jerry* and of Mr. Vertembrex writing of him in his journal-book."

"Ay, ay," said Obadiah, "I was a-telling you as how Mr. Vertembrex took in hand to be much in company with Jerry for to learn all he might as to what manner of creature he was, a-coming up out of the sea so oddly, and did write of him in his journal-book; for he did write hearty."

"This is it," said Mr. Huxtable to the Captain, "that I saw in the journal, and intended to have looked at again, as I told you; for I do recollect seeing the word *sea-savage*. We will search it out anon. But was Mr. Vertembrex able to hold any converse with this sea-creature?" (said he, turning himself again towards Obadiah). "Had he any faculty of speech? But hold! if this Mr. Vertembrex be the same as the person I found on the abandoned ship, he could not speak with him if he was in that condition he is now in; for he seems not able to utter a word. Had he, then, his speech when he was with you, and did he demean himself like an ordinary man?"

"Ay, your honour," said Obadiah, "he was ordinary enough when he was aboard with us, like you and me (begging your worship's pardon), although much given to writing, as I have told you; and what can possibly have changed him like to what he is now, I knows not, nor has the least notion of, any more than I can tell you what is become of the rest of the crew. May be something has befallen him beyond natural, and he has seen what nobody ought; and, as I do recollect, I have heard tell of an antic dumb sailor as was taken up driving at sea in a ship's boat and set ashore on the India coast, but what did become of him I knows not. Also, I mind me of an ancient sea-saying; which is that *the sea yields not up his bone save to him as never after can divulge that it had*."

"Why, what do you mean by that?" said the Captain, who much affected proverbs, apophthegms, and the like.

Mr. Huxtable himself provided the interpretation (which will be sufficiently clear to the reader), and quickly put Obadiah under way again.

But it were tedious to proceed further in such a homely vagabond style; which we ourselves had scarce been able to hear with patience, if the matter had not so nearly concerned us. To be brief, accordingly, Obadiah told us that Mr. Vertembrex contrived to hold discourse with that sea-savage in some degree by the means of signs; that it could speak, after a manner—or, at any rate, utter sounds; and that he understood it very well; that, in appointing him as his emissary to Mr. Huxtable, his Captain (that is the captain of the pirate ship) gave him leave to take *Jerry* (as he called the creature) along with him to England; that it had conceived a particular regard for him, and would perform his bidding exactly in every article.

He did intend to have shown it for a sight in England, as Captain Dampier did his *painted man*, Prince Jeoly, and after to sell him. But being come with him to Bristol, he was afraid what notice such a remarkable exhibition might draw upon himself, who, as being a pirate's man, was not sedulous of public observation.

Upon taking up his lodgings, therefore, which he found at the *Shakespeare* tavern, beside the court where I delivered him Mr. Huxtable's letter, he was more in care to conceal the creature than to show him, and absconded him as much as he possibly could in his chamber in the inn.

He ought now to have performed his Captain's errand; but a foolish fear, or diffidence, of meeting Mr. Huxtable came over him, being, as he said, quite *without his element* on land (so that Mr. Huxtable was in the right in the conjecture that he proposed to me at the farm in regard to Obadiah's sending the letter by me); and he kept delaying day after day, regaling himself at the inn till pretty near all his money was spent. In this time, he fell in with Mr. Falconer, who was wont to come and sit nightly in the tavern.

"There he would sit" said Obadiah (for I continue in his style, as near as I am able) "with a cup before him, and never a word nor a look at anybody. We smelled the sea on his coat, for all his whey face—me and my gossips—and took him for the mate, or second mate, of some vessel lying in the river; and the look of him was like a cold chill mizzling rain. None of us ever spoke to him. One, coming new to the inn, would speak to him, passing the time o'day, or the like, but had such a mopish return as made him sheer off quick, lest, lying anyways aboard of him, he should be drawn down presently into a deep dump.

"Howsoever, a-coming in one evening, and stepping to my place near the hearth, I saw him lift a finger and beckon to me. *What, do you take the face to be a-beckoning to me?* says I to myself, *as if you was on your quarter-deck? I'll strike before I goes to ye!*

"So, I sits me down, and calls for rum; and my gossip pulls out his box and counters; and, all the time, while we was a-casting of the dice, I was sensible he observed me; and, looking up, his eyes did come turning on me, so as it give me a shog, your honour, like as they would pluck me from my seat on the bench. All on a sudden, scarce knowing what I was acting, I rises up after a cast, with no care how the dice fell, and betook myself to beside where he sat.

"*I have a word for you in your ear*, says he, and makes a motion to me to sit down by his side.

"So I sits me down; and he says in my ear: *Make no delay, but get you gone; for there's a watch and observation on ye.*

"*How know you this?* says I, being set all on a tremor.

"*Spend not the time with questions,* says he, *unless you will be taken; but bethink you where to abscond yourselves. Seek out some place and lie close until the ship sails.*

"This gave me a turn too, your worship, seeing as it plainly showed he knew I had Jerry with me; so I resolves to do what he admonished me. And, as to a place to abscond into, by good luck, as it chanced, I had gone for to spy out your worship's farm on the day previous, and so bethought me of the mill which I took partic'ler notice of, being empty, and wondering why it should be.

"So I tells Mr. Falconer (not as his name was beknown to me then, but not till after), and he answered that I should remove therein with Jerry no later than the morrow night; and, being in, neither on us should once issue forth by day, but only by night, and that only on dark nights. *But how shall we do for victuals?* said I. *Rest you easy as to that,* says he, *I shall provide your wants.*

"It needs not to be a-telling you, your worships, 'twas but a dismal look out for a poor misfortunate man such as I was—nor yet any man else, for that matter—and, if I goes for to take along with me aboard the mill a store of rum, 'tis no more than what another would ha' done in the like predicament, as any sailor would bear me out. And so I did, your worships; which near brought about our ruin, a-setting the mill afire, as your worship was witness—I mean, of the fire; not of the misfortunate cause. Mr. Falconer provided us with supplies, coming in the middle of the night, both beef and bread, and good store of salted herrings for Jerry; for he seemed to know without my acquainting him that Jerry did feed on fish.

"I am not able to tell you what Mr. Falconer was concerned in my matters, to deliver me by admonishing me in the inn, nor yet how he came to know of me and Jerry. 'Tis all perplexity and mists and darkness. I was delivered safe from the town bailiff, or whoever was after me, and more I cared not. I have no headpiece for such puzzling gear; and Mr. Falconer would tell me nought. He admonished me that your worship would forbid my having Jerry aboard with me, very like, when the ship sailed, and that I should abscond him on the ballast, if I desired to have him with me (as I did) and that he would assist me—"

He broke off; for the Captain began to rail at Mr. Falconer, calling him by every opprobrious epithet he could set his tongue to.

"I have ever known him for a rogue," cried he, transporting himself in his chair. "Ha! a rogue, with his snivelling whey face. A rogue! a fox! a snipe! Assist you, would he? Ha! I'll—"

He started up while he spoke, and made a pace toward the door; but Mr. Huxtable prevented him.

"Sir, I beseech you," said he, lifting up his finger. "First let us hear this man to an end. Then will be a time to deal with Mr. Falconer. Let us learn all we possibly can; we are sufficiently in the dark. Indeed, I had thought you had desired it no less than I."

Upon this, the Captain sat down again, surlily chafing and murmuring, and Mr. Huxtable bade Obadiah to proceed.

"Well, your worship," said he, "I don't know but that I have much more to tell'e. I had set my heart on taking Jerry along with me in the ship, though I was willing to have sold him afore; and, if you enquires of me how that was, I couldn't tell'e. I don't go for to profess myself to be one of your saints. There an't much of the *milk of human kindness* (in a manner of speaking) in me; and I don't know as I ever saw a dog, or a cat, or a ship's boy, but what I'd a—but that's from my course" (said he, perceiving Mr. Huxtable to grow impatient at this tedious talk). "What I was telling you was as how I had set my heart on taking Jerry along with me aboard the ship. So Mr. Falconer gives me a hint, a night or two before the ship sailed, to take him along with me to the river for to get him aboard and stowed away in the peak, and tells me he had gone to work with the two men that lay aboard, keeping watch. I asks him, had be bribed them. He told me no; for that was to have run too great a hazard to have endeavoured to have bribed them, since they was Mr. Huxtable's men, body and soul, alow and aloft.

"*I have not bribed them,* says he; *but I have drugged them,* and tells me how he put on the clothes and habit of a common huckster and sold them some bottles of rum with poppy in it. This made me laugh hearty; though he did tell it to me with his face as solemn as a parson at a funeral.

"So we sallied forth, Jerry and me, towards the river. But I mistook the hour (having, as I do own, drunken too much liquor), so as it was too soon in the night. And also, your worship, I had kept no look out at the window, as I was wont to do, spying on your goings out and your comings in (asking your worship's pardon). So, when we comes to the river, and was a-going for to go aboard, we nigh run foul of you; for, it seems, you was come aboard the ship with this-here young gentleman.

"Howsoever, I learned my error in time. On a sudden, I hears voices, which was not of the watch, and sees a glimmering light a-coming up the hatchway. Back runs I in the darkness, never taking thought of Jerry. But he, beholding the bright lantern, immediately makes a dive in the river, as his instinct told him, belike, being such a water-creature. For, this be a very curious particular in Jerry, your worship, that he can live nigh as well in water as in air, remaining below a powerful long time on end, so as you would think he was never going for to come up any more; which was one of his wonderful strange performances I was a-going to turn to account if I had showed him for a sight."

"How long can he remain under water?" asked Mr. Huxtable, interrupting him. "A full minute? Two?"

"A minute, your worship!" cried Obadiah. "Why, I have known him ride it out full half an hour; as my old shipmates could be witness what saw it on a day when we lay becalmed, for we delighted to see him perform it, your worship, and would give him rewards such as he fancied—an old montero cap, a gaudy handkerchief, and the like. Sometimes we was nigh wearied out with watching for him, he stayed so long below, and concluded he was certainly drowned, or else was gone quite away. Sometimes he would bring us back something from the bottom; and look 'e here, your worship, here be a cur'osity for ye, if it be no offence I does in a-proffering it to you. This be a present from the bottom of the sea, fetched up by Jerry; and I hopes, if you will pleasure me by accepting of it, as it will bring you good luck."

While he spoke, he pulled from his belt a knife of a very curious figure and fashion. 'Twas of stone, being all of a piece. The blade was wrought in the pattern of a long slender leaf; and at the heel of the haft, or handle, was a cross within a ring, with other strange devices about the middle. This he gave to Mr. Huxtable, making a comical scrape; while the Captain and I rose up from our chairs to obtain the nearer view.

"That's a great cur'osity, your worship," said he; "and, though you was to search through the whole world, I doubt you would not find its like; which inclines me to think your worship will not be unwilling to accept of it."

This capacious offer a little stumbled Mr. Huxtable; who at first (as plainly appeared) was going to treat it as an impertinence. But, after a moment's pause: "I see not why I should not accept of it," said he; "and 'tis, as you have said, a great curiosity. Well I shall set a value on it," said he, with kind and gracious accents; which curiously contented Obadiah so that he stood smiling like a great child.

But, while he spoke, there came a sound of our men running together on the deck; and, as it ceased not, but rather increased, Mr. Huxtable bid me go and see what the matter was.

I went in haste, being exceeding unwilling to lose what more Obadiah might divulge while I was gone.

When I came out on our deck, the moon was set, and the stars shone flickering, like wasted candles in a solemn hall; wherein the noise and hubbub our men set up seemed in the nature of a profanation.

They stood all crowded on the larboard side, and I thought at first they were but embroiled about some trifling dispute; but what was my astonishment, upon going nearer, to behold Mr. Falconer and that little mute man being haled hither and thither in the midst, while some endeavoured to drag them to the side, others as violently opposed to have prevented them.

But, as I stood staring on them, the tumult, on a sudden, subsided and fell quiet, while I heard the voice of that ancient pious sailor upraised in a gentle mild remonstrance.

"Sirs," said he. "Sirs, I beseech ye! Here is a wicked violence that you do. What! would you call down a vengeance upon you? I charge you immediately to cease and give over, in the name of heaven!"

But the boatswain, who discovered himself to be the prime mover in this assault, begun to call upon them, with wild scurrilous oaths, not to take any notice of the *old prating loon* and not to let go of the *Jonah devils; these hand-in-hand damned wizards, that had bewitched us, and the ship, and the flat ocean.*

"Overboard! overboard! and let them swim!" cried he, in an access, "or let the devils, their masters, bear them up! Else, let the sea swallow them, swallow its own physic! take physic of what hath bewitched it! Bear a hand, all," cried he, gripping hold on Mr. Falconer by the shoulder, and begun to horse him along with violent heaves.

But the ancient seaman spoke again.

"Beware how you despise my warning!" said he. "Beware!" and the word was taken up and repeated by the rest as with one voice, so that it swelled in the night with a solemn and roaring sound.

This quite conquered the boatswain; and, unhanding Mr. Falconer, he turned away, murmuring. The rest dispersed in several knots, being now as quiet as they were before angry and embroiled; and the mate and Mr. Vertembrex, left standing alone in the middle of the deck, went diverse ways; Mr. Falconer composing his coat (being dragged half off his back), but after such a careless negligent manner, you might have thought this wild business had been none of his matters, no more than if those that had so mishandled him had been but elementals—as winds and waters; and, indeed, like that little mute man, he did demean himself as if his thoughts were removed far inward and not minding outward happenings; which was the strangest thing of all.

At this juncture, Mr. Huxtable came out on the deck, being followed by the Captain and Obadiah, and was acquainted by me with what had befallen.

He heard me with an anxious and haggard countenance, glancing his eyes at the Captain, careful, as I suppose, to prevent him from acting something outrageous; although I rather think the Captain was more contented than offended by our men's violence to Mr. Falconer. He muttered some angry expressions, as that they were a *mutinous crew*, and the like, but not unreadily assented to Mr. Huxtable when he said, that, since the men dispersed before they came up, he thought they could compose this affair into something less heinous than a mutiny.

"For, although" (said he) "it should be so held in a legal court, yet we must consider, as reasonable men, what the magistrate could scarce take cognisance of—I mean, the panic terror in which they were cast by the coming of that monstrous creature. Let us, therefore, have them to the rail, and do you speak to 'em; for we ought to compose this matter forthwith, and not leave them in an apprehension that we shall hold them guilty of mutineering."

"'Fore George, sir!" cried the Captain, "I think you're the more accustomed to speak to them yourself."

"Very well, sir," answered Mr. Huxtable, "and so I will, if you will give charge to get them together."

The Captain, hereupon, called to Mr. Falconer to have our men assembled on the main deck; where, from above, we presently beheld them; a sullen and rueful crew, standing silent, or murmuring, with the light of dawn, which begun to break, shining cold and ghastly upon their upturned faces.

Mr. Huxtable begun to speak; and sufficiently pacified their spirits; but what expressions he used with them I am not able to set down; for the faculty of my mind was overfull, so that, as I believe, I actually slept, standing supported against the barricade; nay, my recollection is but vague of how I afterward did get to my cabin and take up my repose.

CHAPTER XVIII

Quest for the Rock Pillar: Appearances of Lights in the Sea

It is not strange but that, upon recalling to my thoughts those extraordinary surprising events of the past day, when I awoke in the morning, I at first took them to have been scenes in a dream rather than actual occurrences.

I dressed myself quickly and went aloft, and found the weather to be unchanged, our ship continuing to bear all the sail we could make. The air came hot and close, and the sea appeared uncommon dark, the colour of a sloe, or damson, under a dark, cloudless sky.

Our men were quiet and orderly, but yet, methought, somewhat sullen too. One of them told me, upon enquiry, that Mr. Huxtable and the Captain were gone to breakfast in the cabin; whither, accordingly, I made my way.

They took no notice of me upon my entry, Mr. Huxtable seeming to brood in his mind while he ate, and scarce hearkening to the Captain, who was speaking with a vehement tone.

"I shall not conceal my opinion," said he, while I sat down, "that it's nothing else but plain unreason and downright gross superstition; and, if you was to meet with such an extravagant windlestraw notion among our men, you would rebuke 'em heartily; for I have heard you reproving 'em for much less. Have you considered what it might work upon them? for they will not remain ignorant of it, be sure! They are too apt already to be taken with such moon-stuff. What! do you observe the prompting of a sort of scribbling loon? Sir, I protest, I wonder how you can."

Mr. Huxtable returned but a short answer, speaking gruff in his beard; and the Captain, continuing in the same tenor, discovered to me what had occasioned him so much displeasure, being Mr. Huxtable's desire that we should cruise about in search of that *Rock Pillar* named in the mute's writing, which he thought might be some small island lying unknown in these parts of the ocean.

At last, the Captain, put quite out of patience by Mr. Huxtable's brief replies, absolutely demanded that he should leave this extravagant resolution and keep the ship on her proper course.

Mr. Huxtable asked what he conceived that might be, seeing that we had not arrived the appointed rendezvous but found the pirate ship with no one on board save Mr. Vertembrex only. He answered that it should be for the nearest place on the India coast, to replenish our provisions and fill our water-casks, and thence return to England; or, if he wished to go on in his quest, we should cruise about, and prosecute enquiries up and down the coast, where provisions could be had at some places and in any ships we happened to meet at sea. To which Mr. Huxtable answered that we should do this also, but first prosecute a vigilant search for the *Rock Pillar*; "which, as I told you" (said he), "I have a secret persuasion we shall find, and that it's very material to my quest. But, be this how it may, I shall not be content to leave any, the most outlandish, obscure chance untried. This, therefore, we shall perform, and see what will come of it."

He ended with a peremptory tone; but the Captain started up from his chair, oversetting his glass.

"See what will come of it!" cried he, with his face fiery red and the veins starting on his forehead. "'Fore George, sir, I will tell you what will come of it, and that is, I'll serve no more in quality of Captain aboard your ship! I deliver up my office; I'll not be gainsaid and subordinated by a stark wool-gathering loon. Let him be your Captain! fit captain for such a goose chase!"

With this, he ran raging out of the cabin, shutting the door after with all his force.

Mr. Huxtable sat still in his chair; and, though I could not see his eyes, being bent down upon the table, I saw from his stern brows and clenched fist that he was in a great anger. Nay, I was sensible of it, as on a past occasion, as a huge, heavy-hanging cloud, which every moment might break with thunder.

At length, with a massy vehement movement, as if he shook off a weight, he rose up, and betook himself from the cabin; whence I followed him out to the deck.

I was surprised, upon stepping forth, to see how dark the heavens appeared, even darker than before, though clear sky, the sea looking almost black. Yet, what was still more remarkable, the light of the sun, which seemed to be dissolved (for I could scarce descry its rim), was no less than on any the brightest day; else, indeed, it had been apparently darker in the cabin, which it was not; and our ship, in all her sails, masts, and spars as well as the unshadowed spaces of the deck, did shine very bright.

There was, methought, something more than ordinary in it; and I told Mr. Huxtable my apprehensions. He answered that it certainly looked strange, but that he saw nothing to be disquieted at.

"But may't not signify," said I, "a dreadful storm? What, if it should suddenly gather and break upon us, with our ship carrying so much sail?"

"We shall be ready for it," said he; "but now, you see, there's not a cloud in the sky."

"Give me leave, sir," said I; "I doubt that the Captain will be too angry to take proper precautions and order the ship."

"And do you think I am all so simple as not to take care against that?" said he sarcastically. "But come! I am afraid you have not taken proper care, of late, with your Latin; and, if I was a severe preceptor, you might have occasion to fear another sort of storm! Go, bring me my *Tully* from my cabin, and I shall hear you read over that place in the *De Senectute* treating of those lofty evidences of the immortality of the soul; for I would fain see them well implanted in your mind, if nothing else."

While I went, I saw the Captain coming down the deck. His look was moody; and he saluted Mr. Huxtable, with a sullen glum tone, but in what words, or sense, I could not hear. However, when in half an hour, having finished my task, I returned, I saw them pacing side by side in discourse of low and friendly tones. I did hear Mr. Falconer's name mentioned once and twice, but could not hear the matter; for they broke off immediately I was come near. It was come into my thoughts that certes, by this time, they had interrogated Mr. Falconer as they intended to have done.

The sultry hot wind held intermittent all this day, though it can scarce be called a wind, it was so light: yet our ship just steered; the sea and sky continuing of the same extraordinary strange complexion, darkening towards noon even more pitchy blue and purple and umber.

Thus we held on our random course, keeping always a sharp look out for the *Rock Pillar*; and Mr. Huxtable promised a handsome large reward to the first man that should spy it. I doubt not but that my readers will marvel as much as I did, how a man so reasonable as Mr. Huxtable was, should take into his head to prosecute such a chimerical wild notion, as (by all appearance) this seemed to be; yet far otherwise in the event, as in no distant hour, we did learn.

The odd seascape was more and more uneasy to me, tempering my thoughts (by how much I can express the tenebrous and mysterious imaginations that came over me) to its own hue and element. Nor the less, by all appearance, was it disquieting to our men; who, judging by some low muttered discourse I heard, did take it for a prodigy, if not for a portent. As for Obadiah, I observed he held himself aloof from the rest, sauntering about the deck with a sour countenance and such a surly hang-dog demeanour as ordinarily, no doubt, had chafed them and run him into some angry dispute.

I did often during that day look narrowly to see if I could spy a ship; which I thought might have availed to take off the uneasy forebodings that oppressed my soul. But I never did; and, in the state of mind in which I was, I verily believe I should have been astonished if I had. For all things appeared phantastical and strange, as if we were gotten into some supernatural region, and anything so ordinary as a ship appearing on the sea had been as if something solid and substantial should be thrust forth, on a sudden, in the habitations of shades and phantoms. Nay, for all our deck and masts and sails did shine so bright, the day had in my apprehension the quality of night. The dusky heavens appeared of a smoky tincture, bringing to my remembrance that gaudy Spanish church which I saw when I was a child, all fragrant with the fuming censers; and, at the recollection, my thoughts passed in the manner of a dream to that morning when, after making my escape from the academy, I awakened and beheld the gay meadow and the blue flowers in the wood.

This lively excursion a little refreshed my thoughts; but, a drowsy fit coming over me presently, I lay down on the deck beside the bulwarks, having a coiled rope to rest my head; whereupon the low ambiguous voices of our men, and the small sounds the wind made in the sails and cordage might probably have disposed me to sleep. But I lay in a sort of apathy, having an eye open to outward happenings.

Towards sunset, I rose up and begun to rove about our deck. The sea and sky continued of that strange complexion of dark violet, but lighter in the west about the declining sun, appearing of a hard glowing consistency, like amethyst, streaked with carnelian.

There was, I thought, an unwonted strange hush upon our ship. No sound of voices—no, not a murmur—among our men; and they stood, or moved about, after a sluggard slow manner, as if they had been drugged.

The sun was sunk; the stars appeared, yet lacking of that wonderful golden lustre in which we commonly saw them since we came into these parts. The light wind now quite died away; and a mist arose; which increased, but only so as to cast up a veil beneath the already dimmed stars; and then it appeared as a blue vapour in the air. It hung from side to side across our deck in pearl-like wraiths, wherein our men appeared to stand enchanted.

Some time in this day I took an occasion to inquire if Mr. Huxtable had learnt anything from Mr. Falconer on the topic of Obadiah's narrative. He told me, no: that he had endeavoured it more than once, but that the least mention of those obscure matters did so work upon Mr. Falconer's mind as to bring him nigh into the very state and image of death.

I went to rest; but I could not sleep, any more than I could that night when, upon going aloft, I was taken by our men for a ghost; and, as it was then, so now: I had lain not long in this wakeful state when

I felt a sort of inward prompting to rise and go on deck; and, though in a manner I did conclude it was nothing else but phantasy—which, no doubt, it was on the former occasion also—yet I presently rose up and went aloft in my long cloak.

'Twas a clear starry night, the light wind having revived and the mist dispersed; and pleasant it was to come into the cool air, to behold the stars, and the crescent moon, goldenly shining in the sky, that was the soft velvet dark colour of a pansy.

I looked about me, but saw nothing beyond ordinary on our ship. The watch appeared quiet and orderly; and, under the poop, the rest lay on their mattresses, as Mr. Huxtable, who always had a great care to the health of our men, since we came into these torrid parts desired that they should do, instead of lying in the close forecastle. Mr. Falconer (being now in his ordinary health) stood on the quarter-deck near the helm.

While I observed him, he turned his head, looking sharply and of purpose (as it should seem) out to sea over our starboard bow; and, on glancing my eyes that way, I thought I espied something in the waves that glistened as pearl-shell, and immediately afterward other the like appearances—three, four, or five of them—all close beside of each other, as it might be a knot of dolphins or porpoises swimming: and so, indeed, I took them to be, and that appearance of shining the effect of sea-fire, whereby the water, especially in these parts of the ocean, being troubled—as by the plying of oars—is made to appear by night all of a silver shine.

The appearances presently vanished away; and then I thought of them no more. But they were not porpoises, or dolphins—no, nor any the like sea-fishes or sea-beasts. If I had but known what they were (and also some other things besides), I had not been ignorant why Mr. Falconer kept on looking in that quarter, as he did, where they appeared. The time was not long distant when I learnt what a dark, terrible significance there was in what I beheld thus, as in a glimpse, in this my second night-adventure to our deck; which I returned to bed accounting so little remarkable.

It will appear in the sequel of my narrative; which not to hinder, I'll jump the succeeding day, in which nothing worth remark fell out (the weather continuing as before) until the evening: when that befell which I know not how I can relate, or how my readers will be able to receive, although I should be furnished with the art and the force of a masterly writer.

CHAPTER XIX

Mr. Huxtable's Philosophy

When I went in to supper, I found the Captain had quite recovered his temper and ordinary spirits. Nay, we had not sat long but he grew exceeding merry, relating some gaudy japes, sometimes descanting on his grand acquaintances (as he thought them) in manner already described.

Mr. Huxtable was also in brave spirits: though not boisterous gay like the Captain; yet to that degree I had never known him in before, or thought he could be. He seemed like to one drunken; yet, nevertheless, in the possession of a clear reasonable mind. That sad overshadowing sorrow was absent from the wrinkles in his forehead, and his eyes did shine with a sort of sunny brightness.

I inclined to set down this exaltation of the Captain and Mr. Huxtable (however you may think me phantastical) to Mr. Vertembrex being present with us, feeling in myself an happy correspondency and elation of my soul; and, to my surprise, Mr. Huxtable expressed the same opinion.

This was after Mr. Vertembrex retired to his cabin (as he did always after supper, when the cabin-boy entered to clear the board) and while the Captain, having spent the foolish quiver of his wit, drunk his wine, and smoked his pipe of tobacco, was fallen into a doze.

"Whenever I am with him," said he, of the little mute man, "I am sensible of an upraising and irradiating of my spirits, as if he bears about with him a sort of supernatural lantern."

"So is it also with me," said I.

"What, do you feel it?" said he. "That's strange. We have some profit, then, of this odd companion. It cannot be but for some secret virtue, or efficacy, that he has. I do never cease to marvel what his state is, and how he came to be in it; for if Moon does not lie—and I see not why he should in such a point—he was not so when he was with those pirates. Saw man ever the like of one that seems to know, yet, notwithstanding, to be not sensible of what he does; eats, sleeps, goes his ways, as if he was performing actions in a dream?"

"He is like to one of those shades in the old Greek underworld," said I; "but yet he is too cheerful for that."

"That's true," said he; "but, methinks, Mr. Falconer would make a fitter picture to such a frame. Now, in this somnambulary state is he cognisant of another life within him to which the outward bears the semblance of a dream?"

"It must be, then, but a childish life," said I, "to take his pleasure in threading glass beads. It brings to my thoughts Mr. Falconer and his little ships; which is a boy's business, too; though a boy would never be able to contrive such outlandish strange effigies as he makes at their bows."

"'Tis wonderful strange—" said he, and stopped, falling off into a muse. "I see not how it can bear on the matter," said he, at length; "but those expressions in the mute's writing—*sunflower, summer-house, cinnamon and blue*—did conjure up old childish recollections in my thoughts—of a house and a spacious large garden and shrubbery in a village near Deal, wherein, being about six years old, I abode two or three months with my parents.

"This garden abounded with all manner of flowers and shrubs and fruit trees, and I passed my days there with delight; but what principally engaged my mind and now enchants my recollection, was a large summer-house standing in the wall (being shaped in a circle that enclosed the garden); and this summer-house, mark me! had windows stained blue and cinnamon.

"Many years after, when I was come to years, having occasion to make a journey into those parts, I went to view the place. The garden, though of a good bigness, looked much smaller than I had imagined it to be, which is a common experience in revisiting the haunts of our childhood; but the summer-house was not diminished one jot. The hour was nigh sunset; and, while I stood looking upon it from a cornfield without the wall, the dark blue pane over above my head cast a smouldering gleam.

"Another thing of delectable recollection which the mute's writing recalled to me, was the sunflowers in this garden, with their great flaming discs, caked with gold, and their honey-sweet fragrance."

"What can be thought, or conjectured, from this," said I, "unless a mere accident? But can it be that Mr. Vertembrex was inditing—or, at least, intermixing—some recollections of his childhood?"

"Well thought on, Will," said he. "Indeed I find you apt; and it's true such a notion entered my mind, though, perhaps, too phantastical. But, be this what it will, whether or no he was recalling his childhood, he has strangely hinted at mine.

"This topic of childhood and the enchantment it casts, has powerfully worked in my thoughts, and was the ferment of my philosophy when first I became sensible of its loss and what a brave glittering robe was fallen from me into the past. It's my first chapter of *Genesis*, which, in that story of lost Paradise, is a grand fable of the beginning of our life in this world; when we are innocently happy, or, as I may express this harmonious state, *happily whole*. There is as yet no rift to set body and spirit out of tune in their jangling spheres, and the elements are so mingled in us as that we may truly be called, in those eloquent words, *living souls*, and, like Adam, before (in a manner of division from himself) there was created his female, *Eve*—nay, before ever he knew the need of such a complemental mate.

"I know not if you will be able to understand me, Will," (said he, smiling on me), "though I have found you of capacity to understand such pieces of philosophy—yea, beyond your years! and some things that are obscure to you, being well planted now, may grow up when you are older. I shall read to you something out of my book. You did not know—did you?—that I was writing a book."

Hereupon, after glancing his eyes at the Captain, who continued to slumber, he went and took from his desk a bundle of papers, which he set upon the table. Thereupon, having turned to a place, he begun as follows:

"In that sweet age—I mean of childhood—the light shines in the soul, as it were all of a crystal without flaw, kindling like rays in all external things. Intellect and sense are homogeneal, and to think and be sensible of are as one function. Like unto the Angels of whom Milton sang, *All heart,* we live, *all head, all eye, all ear, all intellect, all sense.* But when that sad division is accomplished (sad in its issue, though far other in its end, or object), the bright mould begins to cloud; whereof the effects, at that change signified by the eating of the tree standing in the centre of the garden, are not only the mortal perception of good and evil, but also the parting in twain of all things into false and contrary faces.

"Henceforth we're not only banished from our paradise, but, in one way, from the whole world; of which, like to a paradise, or enclosed garden (which is the meaning of the word), we behold but the outside. Our eyes are open—but not that internal eye that's brighter than the sun. We have taken Psyche's lamp, dropping hot oil, and the god is departed."

He broke off, to ask me if I understood what he read. I answered that I understood it very well, except *Psyche's lamp* and the *god that was departed*.

"Nay, I had forgot that you did not know," said he. "This is an elegant Greek fable of love's young paradise and its loss, and is not unworthy to be compared to the other—I mean, the story of Eden—though in a lower clime. Nay, in one way, it's the more perspicuous and hath the greater latitude, as you shall hear; for I have related it in another place."

Having turned the page, he read:

"Psyche was a king's daughter, charactered as a small winged maiden, or else as a butterfly, to signify, as I suppose, a soul lifted light on love's pure air. But the goddess, Aphrodite, being jealous, sent her son Eros, or Cupid (as his other name is), with intent to singe those dazzling wings by the kindling of a mortal flame—a design, as it fell out, that quite miscarried. For no sooner, hath Eros beheld her, but himself becomes enamoured of the beauteous maid; and, instead of causing her to love a mortal man, he bears her off to a palace in a vale of Paradise, where they lived with delight.

"But this Paradise also had its prohibition. Psyche was strictly forbid to look upon Eros with her mortal eyes. Neither did she desire to do so: having him ever in her immortal sight, what could she wish for more?

"She had continued thus happy, but that, yielding to her sisters' envious tongues, that aroused her curiosity, one night, taking a lamp, she stole into the chamber where Eros lay sleeping. Whereupon, while she gazed all trembling, a drop of hot oil spilled upon the shoulder of the god; who, awakening, and upbraiding her disobedience, immediately betook himself away, leaving her all forsaken.

"She could no longer continue in that void paradise, where everything she looked on cast a reflection of her dear lost joy; the bright light was more afflicting to her than thick darkness. It was all empty and silent; and sometimes she heard, or thought she heard, the voice of Eros as hollow falling murmurs, vain and lamentable sounds; which drove her out, as a voice more awful, and more dear, had expelled that guilty twain from Eden.

"Yea, even as theirs was, her lot is now to labour; for, wandering up and down searching for Eros in vain, she came, at last to the palace of Aphrodite; by whom she was set to menial service, and finally ordered to descend into the lower world, Pluto's dark region, to fetch a box of beauty's ointment from Persephone, his Queen.

"This heavy and dreadful task she performed; but, on opening the box, sunk, overcome by its odours, to the earth, paying the last penalty of that mortal divided sense, darkly glancing on the outward form; which is beauty's shape of death, in which she appears as by lamplight, when the spirit sleeps: and a sleeping god, thus looked on, is a mortal image (if we rightly consider of it); as, to the eye of faith, the serene look that death casts over a human face, which, in those that have lived worthily is almost divine, may be considered of as an emblem of immortality.

"And to immortality, indeed, Psyche attained, after Eros, no longer able to contain his love, hastening to her, had restored her life."*

While he read, he kept glancing his eyes from the page to observe (in which he was well contented) if I heard and understood. Now, after looking very kindly on me, while I sat silent—being quite out of myself for pleasure—he bade me hear also a *wonderful strange Indian fable*.

"I had it," said he, "from Mr. Falconer. I mean, the plain narrative; but it grew in my thoughts, and I have commented on it."

Thereupon, he read, having turned some pages:

"There was in farthest antiquity a very large and fertile island lying in those parts of the ocean which are off the south side of the island of Ceylon; the inhabitants whereof, like to those of the huge island of *Atlantis*, of which Plato writes in his *Timæus*, were in the first times exceeding prosperous and wise, and of an upright and noble mind, but afterwards fell off from virtue and declined from wisdom.

"They enjoyed at first such a divine infusion of super-eminent vision as cannot be imagined, having converse with that bright world whereof this is but a shadow. They did behold the forms, or bodies, of things through their essential irradiations: thus much more gloriously

---

* *Editor's Notes:*—
(i.) The story of Psyche and Eros is usually held, of course, to illustrate the three stages in a soul's existence—its pre-existence in a state of natural bliss, its travail on earth, and its future state of happy immortality. Mr. Huxtable only relatively identifies the first stage with early childhood, which may be said to be its *reflection*.

   A striking variation on this theme is Blake's poem beginning, "How sweet I roamed from field to field."

(ii.) Mr. Huxtable's comparison of these paradise stories is strengthened by the fact that Nemesis is represented in Greek sculpture as standing behind Eros *holding a twig from an apple tree, her customary attribute*.

substantial. They looked not outwards upon the infinite one way, as from a window, but every way, inwards, as from an aerial sphere; and the utterless sweet fragrance and lively fair, glowing colours of things were the raiment and element of their enchanted souls.

"Love they knew, one with another, without obstacle of corporeal bars: they mingled soul with soul in virtual union, total harmony. Their affections were of the sun; they knew not, nor had occasion to know, its terrestrial and corrosive compound, fire.

"But, in the process of time, this pure and original temper of their souls began to change. Their direct vision with which they enjoyed felicity (for true perception is meeting and union), was turned outwards, and their senses, become mortal, presented to them, instead of real things, but their false and finite shadows. They grew into the likeness of their hearts' imagination; and, in the delusion of isolation consequent thereupon, they appeared to themselves to be compacted into corporeal bodies, and by the very means of these material shadows—by their contact—they thought to attain union. They did conceive them to be really substantial: as though a man should conceit the form, or body, of a picture to be paint and canvas; or that of a poem, ink and paper; which can be destroyed, and yet the poem imprinted again in a hundred such bodies. But the metre and right order of words is the true body, and if it be meddled with, that poem cannot stand. They were taken with appearances, or outsides, erroneously distinguishing for separate principles what were merely contrary appearances—as body and soul, male and female—making imaginary divisions in spiritual entireness.

"In like manner, they separated the quality of beauty, or comeliness, from goodness and truth. They came under the power of pride, greed, and passion; their whole commonwealth, their enchanting dear society, was broken up into the anarchy of warring atoms.

"At last, they began to know and rue their altered state; nor wanted there among them some of understanding that admonished them how they should take in hand to correct this sad deviation by right perceptions, and recover: notably, one—an aged philosopher of a fervent and exalted mind.

"He plainly showed them the nature and operation of their reprobate desires: how empty they were, how false and hurtful: alluring fair in promise; in performance nothing: they only jarred and distempered each particular constitution, and thence the general commonwealth, into anarchy.

"And that concupiscent seeking after union was frustrate in the very means which it took to compass its end; for the sense of touch was not union; nor could the face, or appearance, be divided from the spiritual form (which was also the substance). Bodily propinquity was not spiritual nearness, unless it should be thought that a body, moving any whither, did bear along also the intellectual being; but the spirit moved not, and was not, in the confines of space: its region was ethereal. For there was an elemental region and there was an ethereal region: this being traversed by light, the other by love, which was spiritual light; this was infinite, that was finite; this was eternal, the other temporal.

"He warned them, that, unless they raised themselves from out the illusory and sensual drench into which they were fallen, they would infallibly sink deeper, coming into great darkness, even to a horror.

"This enlightened teacher found many hearers, and probably would have availed, at last, to have brought about a reformation; had not there arose, on the other side, another of as eminent parts and understanding, but of a perverted will, who presented to them another, easier way (as he called it), if not to regain their lost happiness, at the least, to enlarge the scope of their experience and pleasures with new and delightful discoveries.

"The adversary was not old, but in the prime; but laborious days and long nightly studies had fretted his countenance and enfeebled his frame (much unlike the other, who, in old age, had not lost his healthful vigour). He was deeply learned not only in natural philosophy, but also in those obscure and secret forces of the elemental world of which the operations are called magic, and this to a masterly and incredible degree.

"He had searched, not only into the hidden properties of earth, water, fire, and air, but also into the subtlest qualities of light. He had discovered invisible rays of more than chymical efficacy; for these, beyond drugs upon the body, operated upon the soul.

"He asserted that the soul had also its various elements of earth, water, fire, and air, correspondent to those without, and that he was able, by the means of some contrivances he had constructed for the combining and producing of rays having sympathetic correspondency with each element (both within and without), to contract and translate his sensible faculties into the limits of which one of those elements and regions he pleased; whereby he had access into the pure essential of the element outwardly corresponding to this, without any admixture of the other elements, with penetration into the natures and motions of those creatures appertaining to that element, experiencing and enjoying new and unimaginable sensations.

"He asserted, moreover, that certain of these rays discovered many creatures that were ordinarily invisible (being transparent to the eye), of which some were of an incredible oddity and strangeness to amuse and enlarge the mind.

"He gave large assurance, that, if any of the nobles (for by this time they had such nominal dignities) should present themselves for making trial of his engines, he would be able to satisfy them, and through them, the whole populace, that he had not extenuated in any particular of what he had said.

"This novel and spacious declaration, which was uttered from a public rostrum, was received with acclamation by the people and approved by the nobility; some of whom were not backward to engage in the experiment: which, having been done, they all, with common ardour, attested it to have been efficacious and of incomparable excellence and delight.

"Forthwith were means provided for the setting up of those contrivances in many places of the island: to which, at first the nobles, afterward the common people (as they were multiplied), did resort.

"The effects, though not at first apparent, were evil more and more. Those miserable victims were become totally under their power. They sunk from deep to deep; and they who had declined from the love of virtue and integral beauty to be taken with the mere outward form, now yielded themselves to devils: monstrous and abominable imaginations.

"On the natural elements and forces, by disrupting them these iniquitous practices at length brought about an inundation; in which most of the island vanished away beneath the sea, and the small part that remained, being high rock of more than ordinary hardness, declined almost to the level of the waves.

"On this miserable remnant, a few survivors contrived to subsist, though sometimes nigh submerged with the sea waves, by the providence of the fish; and, as there was, constructed in the rock, one of those engines for the producing of rays appertaining to the watery or sea element, so, having regard to the sort of life they were now fated to live, they thought it very commodious; and, tempering and adapting themselves to this element by the single and often employment of the engine, they and their descendants were changed by slow gradations, not only in their minds and souls, but also in their very bodies, to the constitution and condition of a sort of creatures of the sea."

CHAPTER XX

The Inexpressible Light

"Thus far," said Mr. Huxtable, setting his papers in order on the table, "this work of writing I take a deal of pleasure in, though it's a heavy labour, too. You shall help it out with making a fair copy, Will. I know you will be diligent."

He fell silent after this, seeming to muse. The Captain in the meantime slept on, breathing soft and even as a child.

In all this time, while he read, my mind was extraordinary lively clear, to that degree each word and syllable seemed inprinted in my recollection as though 'twas a sort of perpetual wax. I had scarce need to copy them out (for his papers came afterward into my hands, and I design, as my duty is, to publish them to the world).

But now, it is no wonder, the hour being long past my ordinary bedtime, and the cabin close and hot, that those drowsy sounds of the Captain begun to subdue me to their element; so that, while I sat looking on Mr. Huxtable, pondering what he had read, my thoughts passed gradually to a vague lost dreaming. I was just nodding off, with my arms on the table, when I heard Mr. Huxtable utter an exclamation.

"The light!" cried he.

I was immediately sensible upon looking up, that something was befallen more than natural; for the cabin appeared all in a dim light, and yet such, notwithstanding as dazzled my eyes; which, indeed, might be the cause, and not (as it seemed) the effect of the dimness. The lantern burned pale and ghostly, of the transparency of crystal; yet, what was no less remarkable and incredible than that dazzling dimness (by what I can express), the flames of its candles were undiminished.

Mr. Huxtable, in his chair over against me, sat fixed in the aspect of amazement, with a look of exceeding great wonder in his staring eyes. I would have spoken to him; but I could not bring forth one word. I experienced that sense of ineffectual struggle which is a horror in some dreams, appearing to myself to lie under an all-enveloping soft weight, as if the air was become agglutinated into some heavier, supernatural consistence: and, when I rose up from my chair and stepped toward where Mr. Huxtable sat, it seemed not to be myself that laboured thus heavily across the cabin, but my phantom.

It was come into my thoughts that we were dead and that our ship lay drowned at the bottom of the sea; so that I was the less surprised when, upon coming to Mr. Huxtable, and stretching forth my hand to have taken hold on him, though, by the appearance my fingers did approach the place, I could not feel that I touched anything at all. Neither made he the least stir in his posture, nor gave any token that he saw me, but continued, as before, staring wide with that fixed aspect, as if he was under an enchantment.

The reader will think it strange, that, after my endeavours in vain to arouse Mr. Huxtable, I did not repair to the Captain. However, I was distraught to that degree I scarce knew what I did. But this which follows is stranger yet—that, without observing him particularly, I was sensible the Captain continued asleep in his chair; neither did I see anything surprising or beyond expectation in it.

But while I thus stood vainly groping in the air, the tumult of my terror and amazement, on a sudden, abated and sunk, leaving a strange intense stillness, a sense of loneliness and vague uneasy longing, or hankering of desire, for something, I knew not what; which increased until it was as a fretting wasting flame, become more ardent by wanting what it sought.

In the same time, that dim light in the cabin changed—not so as that it appeared more bright, but as having (by what I can express) a sort of internal shining in it, veiled. I felt a sweet rapture, an enthrilling, enchanting joy; while the light (as it should seem) flowed wavering with a charming soft motion into my soul, irradiating and dissolving my bodily sense, setting my spirit free in its element of sunny celestial air.

And now I knew what I before so vaguely divined and longed for. 'Twas the coming of Mr. Huxtable's beautiful lady; and, in a vision of felicity, I beheld her, and was with her in a society inexpressively intimate and dear; and what increased (if that were possible) my joy, I apprehended that Mr. Huxtable was in the same communion: yea, I beheld it, as in a glimpse, in his shining eyes, so changed from what they looked before.

But the vision stayed not long, and was succeeded by very dreadful terrors. For, upon a sudden flickering of the light, the charm was broken; the bright crystalline mould was clouded o'er, distempered with a parching and freezing admixture, like an ague; and I heard a withering ghostly sound. I obscurely understood that the sound was the voice of my grandfather; who appeared before me in a meagre and shrunken feature, with his finger lifted in admonition. He looked on me, pointed downward, and vanished away.

In the same moment, the cabin was full of a sort of hideous creatures, dusky and grim, whom I took for infernal devils, with their high peaked heads, and great glistening dark globular eyes (for I did not immediately bethink me of that sea-monster which appeared in our ship). One of them clipped hold on me with his clammy dank hands, that resembled the flappers of a sea-beast, pressing me to his breast, that was all shaggy and dripping wet like seaweed, and bore me, nigh stifled across the cabin. Others were moving toward Mr. Huxtable and the Captain.

'Twas like some frightful dream; and this the more since the creatures made no sound of speech, only slavered and slubbered, writhing their blubber jaws, breathing short with noisome fishy expirations. Thus, they transported me from the cabin, and out to the deck.

I was at first perfectly dumb with terror, but now I begun to cry—or rather, to shriek out—calling upon our men to save me; for to escape of myself, even to make the least struggle in that soft blubber-like hold, was quite in vain. But there was not a man to see. Our deck, plainly apparent in the bright moonlight, appeared quite deserted.

But now, even upon the shock of this new amazement, I bethought me of that monstrous creature which Obadiah had concealed in our ship, perceiving the resemblance thereto of that which clasped me and the rest that broke into the cabin. I remembered that Obadiah said it was a harmless monster; but this recollection was of brief comfort to me now; for, just as it was come into my thoughts, the creature, on a sudden, leaped, with me in its arms, upon the gunnel. In the same moment, while it stood in the fact of dropping overboard, I beheld a scene, that, of all my exceeding strange experiences in this voyage, is the most lively imprinted in my mind.

This was the appearance, about a cable's length away on our quarter, of a pillar of black rock, rising fourteen or fifteen foot above the waves, that, though they were so small, yet made a high rippling about its base; and, in the parts of sea between, approaching nigh unto it, I saw many dark objects like to the heads of men swimming. Thereupon, the creature sprung with me from the bulwarks.

The shock of plunging through the cold water somewhat revived my courage, and, upon recovering my breath when we were returned to the surface, I was sufficiently in my wits to deliver an indifferent true account to myself of what after befell.

The fish-like creature, clasping me in one arm and swimming with the other, horsed me through the waves, directing its course toward that pillar-like rock. It swum extraordinary quick; and soon we approached near to the rock. I thereupon observed that there rose at the back of it a kind of table-land of the same black stone, but scarce higher than the sea, which run over it in a foaming flood whenever any wave broke upon it.

Arriving this rock table-land, the monster laid hold on the verge, and, with one heave, hoisted up himself and me thereon, setting me down, all breathless, on the wave-washed top.

Thereupon, getting to its feet, it seized hold on me by the collar of my coat, and pulled me up by its side. I immediately observed, at a few paces from where I stood, an orifice in the rock, being regularly square as if it had been made by art, into which the water flowed every time the waves made a breach over the rock. 'Twas about the bigness of a ship's hatch; and that singular strange pillar, standing like the stump of a broken mast, increased the similitude—I mean, to a shipwreck lying low sunk or *water-logged*, (as sailors call it) in the sea.

This appearance hinted me to see for our ship; which I spied a good way off, standing still and shaking her sails, having just fallen into the wind, which was now a little sprung up.

I could take but the one look; for, gripping hold on my arm with his blubber fingers, the creature begun to hale me, all helpless, toward that rock-chasm; and, now, indeed, coming to the verge, and thrust violently over, I yielded myself utterly for lost, scarce able so much as to utter a cry.

Nevertheless, my fall was not far, and the brunt of it was tempered by something less hard than a ground of rock. I was sensible it was the body of a man; but I did not perceive this certainly, and in a moment my senses departed.

CHAPTER XXI

Gorgonian Terror

When I came to myself I was in that weak and apathetic state as scarce to be sensible that I breathed; in which I did continue (as I believe) above an hour, with my nerves and the powers of my mind perfectly listless and numb.

The first thing I really took notice of was that I lay in darkness; which made me think at first—yet without the least sentiments of fear or repining—that this might be the very state of death. Suddenly my sensible or apperceiving faculty revived; and, staring round in a horror, I saw that the darkness was not total, but a sort of dismal tenebrous gloom, which vaguely discovered a large concave place, being about twelve times the size of a castle-tower, having walls of rock and an oval-shaped top like a vault's. But immediately I observed that I lay, upon a thick covering of dry seaweed, on a sort of ledge, which ran all round, projecting from the sides, and also that others lay thereon. I saw them on either side of me, at short intervals, lying, as I lay, on their backs, with their toes toward, and near touching, the verge; and I just descried them, in the obscurity, to be some of our men.

I called to him who lay nearest me with a hushed voice, and then more loud; while I turned upon my belly and crept towards him. But he neither spoke nor stirred.

Coming to him, I found he was the boatswain. He lay with his eyes open in a fixed glare; and at first I concluded he was dead; thence that they were all dead.

It cannot be that the horror and dismay I was in was increased by this conclusion, it was too wrought up already—no, nor that it was abated when I perceived, as I did by setting my hand to the man's mouth, which stood a little open, that he breathed.

I took hold of his arm and shook him; but in vain. The look upon his face was terrible to me. There was some significance in those eyeballs, that glared—or seemed to glare—on me as with some wicked and impetuous joy. My soul recoiled—yea, did start back with a loathing and shuddering motion. I violently turned from the sight. It now came into my thoughts, recollecting how I had been cast down by that monstrous savage creature into the orifice in the rock (as I have related), that this dreadful place was a sort of cavern under the sea.

I was about to look over the parapet, when, a little on one side of me, I spied, in the obscurity, something that moved along upon the verge with a sliding writhing motion. 'Twas a thick, oval, blubber-like object, in colour a darkish red, being (as it should seem) the extremity of a sort of trunk, like the body of a huge serpent; and, staring on it with a horrid fascination, a fearful inquisitiveness, I observed that it was embossed with a sort of cup-like emboluses, or suckers. On a sudden, it vanished over the edge with a faint shuffling sound, leaving me staring on the place where it disappeared.

What it was, or possibly could be, I had no notion; but the sight of it set me in a cold damp; I felt the hair start upon my scalp. Thereupon, drawn by horror's fearful traction, I moved to the verge of the parapet and looked down.

My eyes were now become somewhat accustomed to the gloom; and I found that I was looking, as it might be, into the cavity of a prodigious great well; for, about fifty foot below me in that circular cavern, there was the appearance of water.

Not in that moment, however (I mean, of my looking over the parapet), was I sensible of this—nor, indeed, of anything besides, save only of two enormous round protuberant eyes, being fully as large as port-holes—nay, much larger, with their thick round rims; that appeared to gaze up at me with a baleful and astonied glare. Infernal fury seemed pent to bursting in those eyes, which glimmered like metal in the darkness, and measureless, merciless hate! As if they were the eyes of *Medusa* herself, the sight of them benumbed me all over. I could not stir, nor cry out, any more than if I had been a figure of stone.

But now I vaguely discerned the body from which those frightful eyes stood forth at the upper part—being narrow, but bulging huge and broad below—half raised from out the pool of inky-black water; and, above and around the head (the upper part of the body, rather; for this Terror appeared all body), there did branch forth arms, or trunks, like huge massive serpents, that waved sprawling about the sides of the cavern. I observed that they were covered with emboluses, like to those I saw on that object which moved along the edge of the parapet.

Suddenly I was become sensible of a small scraping sound close under where I lay; and, looking quickly, I spied the extremity of one of those serpent-like trunks, being the same, no doubt, as that which I had seen moving along the rock. It was mounting again, being but a yard below the parapet, with a steady pushing motion. Moved by an urgent prompting beyond my will, I violently cast myself backwards, and lay over on my side; while, arriving the top, the monstrous thing, on a sudden, darted forward, with its suckers wide open like a sort of horrible, eager, gluttonous mouths. It passed but an inch from my shoulder.

Being thus foiled of its object, it held for a moment turning slowly in the air, and thereupon begun searching hither and thither over the surface of the rock. In the meantime, however, with panic expedition heaving myself upon my belly, I was gotten a good way to one side just near that one of our men who lay next along on the parapet—I mean, in the contrary direction to the boatswain: whereupon, being quite overcome with such terrors (which is no wonder), I immediately sunk into a swoon.

I revived (as I believe) soon after; for I appear to myself to recollect opening my eyes—yet no more than a glimpse; and then I fell off into a sleep—but no ordinary, or natural sleep; for 'twas haunted by a dream that was more lively substantial than any mere figment of the brain, and much more terrible.

And I beheld in this prodigious dream, upon a wizard dark ocean, the appearance of a ship; yet in form and fashion much unlike a ship, being oval, as well the deck as the sides of it; neither had it any masts or other sailing-gear. The colour of it was bluish green, glistening as the interior of some sea-shells and wavering with a sort of inner and unearthly lustre. Though I have called it a ship, I vaguely apprehended that it was also (by what I can express) a living creature.

'Twas all shadowy and obscure; but it was become presently a little more clear; and then I observed that the bows, which now perfectly engaged my attention, were of an exceeding strange fashion, and in substance not wooden, or of any hard consistency, but of a corporeal, and sort of inexpressive alluring strange softness. I began to discern the appearance of a shape that was feminine, but not human; yet in what manner differing from human I know not. It was enchanting beyond utterance; than any mortal woman, though it were Helen, or Cleopatra, more seductively and ravishing fair.

I never distinctly descried the appearance (in which, as I apprehend, I was not unblessed); for, on a sudden, there fell a flash as of sulphureous fire, and, on all sides of that obscure and mysterious object there was shot forth monstrous great trunks, that, Gorgon-like, waved curling amidst the clouds.

Thereupon, darkness fell, and horror: thick darkness in which my soul seemed smothered, engulphed in some infernal and abominable element; and, with deadly strugglings and pangs of loathing past utterance, I came to myself.

This, however, was but to pass from one state of horror to another, when I was become sensible in what place I lay.

But that dreadful cavern was no longer silent; for there came from all sides around a sort of confused low humming or roaring, being occasioned, as I soon perceived, by our men who lay therein; and, rising all trembling to my feet, I beheld some of them in the dun light, being all huddled forward, most upon their hands and knees, whilst they stared over the parapet. They looked to be spectators in some obscure and demoniac theatre.

A sort of still and deathly curiosity, on a sudden, succeeded my terror; and, stooping down, I peeped over the ledge.

I dared not, however, look directly below, to have beheld a second time those fiendlike orbs. Yet, notwithstanding, the sight that met my eyes was more actually dreadful; for one of those monstrous great serpent-like trunks, raised aloft in the cavity, was coiled about the body of a man, being not above four or five yards from where I lay. It was Mr. Falconer.

He did not strive, or cry out: constrained (as I did suppose) by the excess of terror and dismay; but when his face, at first averted from me, was, with the slow turning of the trunk, discovered plainly to my sight (for he was lifted quite near me), I beheld thereon much resembling what I had seen on the face of the boatswain, a look of a sort of abounding, extravagant, and antic joy.

It was come into my thoughts, while I gazed, that this also might be nothing else but the figment of a frightful dream. Neither was the sight of our men contrary to such an imagination, they looked not ordinary, but as if they had suffered some unknown, mysterious change; which appeared as well by their postures and movements (when any did move), as in their phantastical odd aspect in the gloom.

By the apprehension and terror they discovered (I thought), it could not be but that they were in a state of sensibility, yet, nevertheless, 'twas not natural.

Now the illusory fiend put it into my thoughts that this was the change of death and the state of damnation; and that we were all translated to a chamber of hell. But immediately upon this horrible persuasion, I recollected Mr. Vertembrex, perceiving how the condition of these lost mariners resembled his.

Scarcely these thoughts had passed over my mind (which was in a moment), and whilst the sight of that incredible horrid enigma of Mr. Falconer's complacent rapt countenance continued before my eyes, but I heard a small rustling sound that seemed to be come from a point higher up on the wall behind me. I turned, and looked aloft; and there, where there appeared a faint brightness, I spied a thing like to a small long snake dangling and descending beside the wall. In the same moment, there came a voice—an unknown voice, high and mellow and pleasant like a tuneful bell—crying:

"Look ye up! Look ye up! Here are ropes for deliverance. Let him that is nearest first catch hold. But beware disorder, or panic striving; else you are certainly lost!"

And, while I stood glaring for astonishment, that voice continued very loud:

"Come, collect your wits! Escape! Save yourselves! Awake! Awake!"

For no man stirred, by what I could observe—nay, nor even at the second, more urgent summons, save only that one of them slightly raised his head; but immediately he lowered it again, returning to the same posture of gazing on that grisly spectacle below; and now I observed that the trunk was gotten lower, bearing Mr. Falconer downwards.

"Miserable men!" yelled the voice. "Are ye, then, quite beyond succour? But you, boy—you hear and understand me, don't you? Try if you can rouse those next you. Come, shake 'em shrewdly!"

I was now a little recovered from my amazement, and I made a shift to perform the bidding; but my limbs trembled so, I was scarce able to move.

I did shake those men—the boatswain and the other—as hard as I could, taking them by the shoulders; yet to no more effect than some low dull muttering of the boatswain, the other continuing perfectly mute.

Thereupon, being bidden myself to ascend the rope, I stepped to it with an urgent panic haste; for I heard one of those dreadful trunks coming scraping by under the parapet. Terror gave me strength; I had else been so weak I had not been able to climb, although on board our ship I had skilled myself to swarm a rope very easy.

Arrived the top, I felt somebody grip hold on my coat-collar with both hands, and hale me up upon the ledge of a small aperture that there was there in the wall.

"Follow me quickly!" said he.

I looked up, and was amazed. It was Mr. Vertembrex!

"You can speak!" cried I, "I thought—"

"Ay," said he hastily, abridging me; "but there will be a time for explanation. Now come!"

"But, Mr. Huxtable," said I with a grievous recollection, "we can't leave him here."

"He is on the ship," said he, taking me briskly by the arm. "Come!"

We stood in a sort of gallery in the rock, that run branching directly from the cavern; and there was a dim light proceeding from the farther end, which was but fourteen or fifteen paces away.

While we passed through, I saw some figures on the walls, being painted a bright lively green, that, by what I did observe in my hasty and distracted course, were odd geometrical representations, being formed with circles, triangles, and the like.

We came to the further end, and issued into a sort of small square shaft, in bright daylight. 'Twas that orifice in the rock-tableland into which the monstrous sea savage had cast me down.

There was a rope hung down by one side, being not above twelve or fourteen foot in depth; and, laying hold on it, Mr. Vertembrex immediately clambered up. I followed suit; whereupon, arriving the top, the first thing I beheld, to my inexpressible wonder, was our ship, lying not above two cables' lengths from the rock.

She lay almost over against the place where we stood, her sails having been shortened to enable her to rest near the wind; and I saw Mr. Huxtable standing at the gang-way, and Giles Kedgley, that ancient greybeard sailor, at the helm.

I stood as in a dream, in the bright sunlight, scarce able to believe I was delivered from that dark abominable cavern; and the sight of our ship was pleasant and comfortable to me; an intimate, familiar, and home-like spectacle, and the sight of Mr. Huxtable was more reviving than I can express.

But a sense of fear came over me, on a sudden, like a chill ghostly shadow; and, in the same moment, I bethought me of that singular pillar of stone, which rose up from the rock at a few paces from where I stood.

I turned to look on it, wondering what possibly it could be. Certainly it was not natural, being too exactly cylindrical and polished smooth. Moreover, it had a sort of square base. Raising up my eyes, I perceived near the top, and bearing seaward, a curious round aperture like a large port.

I had scarce observed this, however, but Mr. Vertembrex diverted my attention.

"Get you aboard the boat," said he. "Make haste, lest they return and take us before we arrive the ship."

I understood he meant those monstrous savage creatures, and wondered where they might be gone, but I did not ask him if he knew; for I catched sight of a man's head—or, to speak exactly, the uppermost part of it—appearing above the verge; and, stepping near, I saw Obadiah Moon in our ship's boat, lying close under the rock.

He looked upon me, grinning broad (whatever he found in the occasion to be so jocular). I jumped aboard; Mr. Vertembrex following. Thereupon, Obadiah thrust the boat from the rock with his oar, and all three pulling away, in a brief time we arrived our ship.

CHAPTER XXII

Mr. Huxtable's Consummation

To my astonishment, and no small mortification, Mr. Huxtable took no notice of my returning to our ship, neither when I waved to him in the boat as we drew near the side, nor even when I was come aboard.

He seemed to be abstracted in a muse, standing looking over the sea toward the rock-island, with his elbows resting on the gunnel; which, at such a juncture as this, I thought, was very singular, even though he did not know from what hazards I was escaped, and from what horrors. I was too proud or—I should say, rather—too sulky to speak to him, thus disappointed of what I had looked for: not only those testimonies of pleasure and affection at my salvation which I naturally expected, but an occasion to unpack my soul (not without some boy-like ostentation) by acquainting him with what I had suffered in that abominable cavern.

I wondered what had befallen him, and how he had 'scaped the clutch of those monsters when they entered the cabin; and suddenly, while I looked upon him, I grew afraid. There was come into my thoughts those mysterious words in the journal-book of Mr. Vertembrex of a light that shone through the cabin walls, and I conceived the notion that this was the same light that shone in the cabin of our ship (certainly it did appear to shine through the walls), and that it had wrought the like effects upon Mr. Huxtable—I mean, stricken him, or enchanted him, after some unknown manner, casting him in the same state as Mr. Vertembrex was in; although (as I had the wit to consider) it did not appear to have had the least operation upon me.

This was a sufficient purge to my umbrage and pride; and I asked him, with impetuous anxious tones, why he did not speak to me.

But he returned no answer, nor gave the least sign of having heard—no, nor when I spoke to him again, catching desperately hold of his arm.

I turned, thereupon, to have spoken to Mr. Vertembrex, supposing he was by my side (for all these various thoughts and motions had passed over my mind—or so it did appear—in a few instants). I had not thought he would have removed from the gang-way without speaking a single word to Mr. Huxtable; but, on finding he was there no longer, I started round, glaring with a panic terror, thinking he might have been witched away, and that I was left alone with Mr. Huxtable only, whose mind was absent, which was all one with his body being absent also—nay, worse, since he would be as a sort of corporeal phantasm unto me. In that instant the nerves of my body quite failed me; and I could not turn my eyes, or my head, to see for Mr. Vertembrex if he was anywhere on our deck.

'Twas as enthrillingly terrible as anything I had known in the cavern (which terrible experiences had reduced me to such a distraught state), though causeless and insubstantial, as, next moment, it proved to be, when I heard the voice of Obadiah hailing from the rigging, that he was mounting up to increase our sail; which put me in mind, that, at the least, I was not alone on the ship; and thereupon Mr. Vertembrex himself called to me to come assist him with hauling up our mizzen-sail.

I was just going, when I observed Mr. Huxtable's aspect to change; and, looking attentively and very affectionately on me, "I thank Heaven, Philip," said he (strangely miscalling me), "that you have been preserved safe. But what is become of our men?" said he, looking about him, tugging convulsively at his beard. "Have they been carried off by—or do I dream? I have not been myself after I looked that demon in the eyes in the cabin. What a struggle was that! More actual than a dream, if it was but a dream. What can have befallen?" cried he, glaring with a distracted eye.

Before I could return an answer, Mr. Vertembrex called to me a second time, with a high impatient tone.

"Why, who is that?" exclaimed Mr. Huxtable, turning about; and, thereupon, set off with me down the deck. As we mounted up the poop-ladder, Obadiah, lying along the topsail yard, cried out that he spied some of those monstrous creatures swimming in the sea; and, looking, I saw twenty or thirty of them in a shoal, being just able to descry them like dark specks in the water off the further extremity of the rock; whither they were plying: which was a lively token to us to make no delay. And, although they did not turn aside, any of them, from their purpose, which was, no doubt, to visit that horrible cavern (whatever occasion had called them away), to have come to our ship; yet, if we had stayed any longer, they might probably come after us when their business was concluded; and, unless we had been well away, have overtaken us (having such a small wind), they did swim so fast. But our ship, clapping on a wind, already begun to move apace.

In the meantime, Mr. Huxtable stood staring on Mr. Vertembrex; who, however, without giving him time to utter a word, desired him with a brisk courteous tone, to assist me with hauling up the sail, and immediately after betook himself to the main-deck; whereupon, with surprising agility, he mounted up the rat-lines.

Mr. Huxtable fell to work without a word, seeming to relapse into his strange muse; in which state he did continue, with brief intervals, unto the end.

If he was spoke to, he returned a reasonable answer, though brief, and with a tone and manner admonishing brevity in his interlocutor also. He seemed commonly, even while he went about his work (which he never stinted, but thoroughly accomplished), to be rapt away in some secret blissful contemplation, or communing, with a look in his eyes like that of a contented lover—yea, of any, the happiest lover, in his most propitious hour.

As for me, I was at first in that bewildered condition, and so weak and crazy (which is no wonder, after what I had suffered), that, if the imperative occasion had not called me to bestir myself, since we were now so few to work the ship, I had been fain to go and lay me down upon my bed.

But necessity may be a brave physician, and no physic, at some times, so efficacious as the complete diversion of our thoughts. So, at all events, it was with me; and those well-nigh incessant labours and continual watchings by day and by night with but little time for sleep and less for meals (which we took singly, at any odd hour, having our victuals always set upon the board), which might have been my death on another occasion—at least, quite wore me out—yet wrought no harm upon me, beyond a fever-chill, that I was ever sensible of after.

However, I am by nature propense to engage in bodily toil and to endure hardness; much more than to suffer the vexed and struggling labours of book-writing: from which cause (as I acquainted the reader in the Introduction) this narrative was so long deferred, until old age, and, being taken in hand, at last, miserably retarded. Now, being come nigh to the close, in view of the wished port—yea, drawing on also to that other desired haven when I shall be able to lay down the great pen of life (which is yet, perhaps, another way, no more than a feather's weight), I do feel my powers of narration to halt miserably benumbed. Therefore, my readers (I hope) will grant pardon to me, though the rest of my book run somewhat short.

Begging the reader's pardon for this digression, I proceed.

The fortunate wind and fair weather continuing, we sailed on six or seven days, generally toward the north-east, but often yawing about; for Giles Kedgley and Obadiah were the only skilful steersmen we had, and Obadiah was commonly befuddled and unhandy with drinking. It was to no purpose that Mr. Vertembrex, as soon as he perceived it, caused all our rum to be cast into the sea, the miserable creature provided himself from some secret store.

Although he took upon himself to order our ship (Mr. Huxtable never signifying the least desire to interpose), Mr. Vertembrex was no master-mariner (I doubt if he knew even how to take the sun; for I did never see him about it); but, by often consulting with Giles Kedgley, he contrived to manage sufficiently well.

This brisk little active man, although I was not sensible since he recovered his speech and ordinary mind, of that illumination of my spirits which I knew before when he was present with me, had yet a heartening and invigorating mien. I wished to have enquired of him about many things, needless to set down, but had few occasions for discourse, since he was commonly occupied with some business or other; and, if it was not concerning the ship, he would be reading or scribbling in a manuscript-book that he bore about with him in his coat-pocket. But on the night of the second day since we left the rock-island, while I kept my watch, the ship sailing smooth (Giles Kedgley being at the helm), he came stepping to me, with his nimble gait, and, after some pleasant salutation, sat him down by my side, and requested me to give him an account of our adventures before we were come to the *Pillar Rock* (as he called it), and also what design Mr. Huxtable had in going this voyage.

I answered that I would relate our adventures very willingly, but, for the rest, although I could tell him, I did not know if Mr. Huxtable might be willing that I should.

"If you was to ask him," said I, "'tis very like he will tell you."

"Nay, perhaps he will tell me when he is more himself," said he; "for, I suppose, he was not always as he is now."

"No," said I. "Do you think he will recover himself?"

"I hope he will," said he; "and perhaps he begins to mend already. This morning he came and asked me if I was not on board a pirate ship, and if there was not a boy held captive there."

"Ay," said I eagerly. "That was his son. Was he aboard your ship?"

"Nay, I do not know," said he. "I cannot see behind me; something has made me blind there, boy; and that's an odd thing, too, if you consider of it—that we look backward in time, and in space afore. Only, Mr. Huxtable's words put into my head what might be glimpses: as if I had about me once a sorry villainous crew. But sure I was ne'er a pirate! You would not take me for a pirate—would you? He! he!" cried he, laughing on the tip of his voice, "it would go hard if I was hanged up in chains, like an innocent babe in his swing, never knowing my crime. Well, I must be merry. As the child was, so is the man; but yet not so, neither. This child was not merry; too happy by far to be merry! I do think I was extreme serious."

"Can you remember a summer-house in your childhood, with coloured glass windows—blue and cinnamon?" cried I quickly, bethinking me of those words he wrote in our cabin.

"Bless us!" cried he, lifting his hands up, "it's my happiest recollection. In Squire Joliffe's great garden. But how came—Ha! ha! I have it. I lay sleeping and talked of it."

"No, you did write it," said I.

"Write it!" cried he. "How can that be? But it's a piece of what you are to tell me. Begin; for, as you may suppose, I am extreme curious."

"So I will," said I; "but first I'll let you know that you were not an ordinary pirate on that ship, but, like Captain Dampier, consorted with such rogues for discovery. You're a naturalist; for your journal-book hath many natural descriptions, as of herbs, trees, fruits, and the like."

"My journal-book!" cried he, "Where is it? Have you it here on the ship?"

I told him it was in Mr. Huxtable's cabin; and, saying that he would ask him for it, he desired me to proceed with my relation; which, accordingly, I did.

After I had ended, he sat awhile in a muse; and thereupon, observing I was very heavy, he told me to go and repose myself; for he would watch in my room.

Two other discourses I had about this time with which it is necessary to acquaint the reader.

One was with Obadiah, the other with Giles Kedgley: enquiring how they two had been preserved safe as well from the power of the light as from the sea-creatures and their cavern.

For Obadiah, however, it can scarce be called a discourse that I had with him; he answered me only with a villainous grimace. I concluded he was neither on our deck when the light shone, nor went aloft after, but lay drunken in the forecastle.

From Giles Kedgley, however, I had an answer indeed. He told me that he saw no light, but that, on a sudden, the sea was changed into a delectable land; a country of enchantment, having great tall trees, whereof the branches, with their massy broad leaves, did cast a cool delicious shade as green as emerald; and all about them, amongst bushes, bearing huge crimson blossoms, there appeared feminine and ravishing forms, all softness and delight, lifting up their alluring arms with a powerful strong enticement to come down to them.

He said that he was exceeding fain to yield, though an old man, and though he had confidently supposed and hoped he had long ago overcome the lusts of the flesh and the seduction of the eyes, and was, indeed, in the very action of clambering over the bulwarks to cast himself incontinently down, as the rest did, into those blissful and delusory bowers, when (as he vehemently affirmed) he *beheld the arm of the Almighty stretched out before him harder than granite*.

The awful spectacle took his soul with such a mighty rapture, and sense of abounding, adoring gratitude as to dispel that inordinate fleshly desire in a moment; whereupon, the airy charm dissolved and vanished away.

These, to the best of my recollection, are his very words; and, indeed, they were lively imprinted in my mind. I am only careful to set them down; not to comment upon them—nor on their substance either. Let them explicate this mystery who can; I leave it to the philosopher.

Proceeding, I come to the time, being on the tenth or eleventh day, in the morning, when the fair wind and weather that we had, was changed to foul, and the wind, after chopping about, grew stormy. Henceforth, our lot, that was sufficiently hard before, was become perfectly wretched.

Hitherto, we did, in a manner, hold a course, designing, at large, to hit the Indian coast, unless, as we rather hoped, we should happen to fall in with a ship at sea; of which the captain, being liberally dealt with, might loan us some of his men, or else receive and convey us, and Mr. Huxtable's treasure to some convenient port. But now, we roved unsteadily under no more than a topsail and a reefed mizzen-sail, not daring to set more sail, lest, the wind suddenly increasing, we should not be able to reduce it sufficiently quick.

On the morning following, we found, to our great discouragement and almost despair, that there was two foot of water in our hold; which, as we had not shipped anything considerable, imported that our ship had sprung a leak. We were not able to find it out (whether or no we could have stopped it if we had); and now it was laid upon us to work the pumps, in which heavy labour, though Mr. Huxtable did discover the strength of two, we were overplied.

All the morning we toiled, except Kedgley, who took the helm; Obadiah (being sufficiently scared) going to work as earnestly as any.

In the meantime, the wind sunk; but, as we found the water in our hold to be rather more than less, it was the less comfortable to us: we were, indeed, in desperate case. But, as Mr. Huxtable's strength had steaded us at the pumps, so the sprightly talk and banter of Mr. Vertembrex assisted us now.

He put us in mind, while we lay, near wearied out, upon the deck about the mast, that there was no condition in the world so miserable, but that there was some good in it to set against the evil.

"For consider," says he, with a dry cast at Obadiah, "how the fear of water may exorcise the devil of rum."

"Ay, ay," said Giles Kedgley, coming to us (for Mr. Huxtable, without resting himself, had taken over the helm); "but the fear of the Lord casteth out terror."

Thereupon, on a sudden, moved with an intense excitement, that made his eyes to shine like lamps, he rehearsed, with lofty and enthrilling accents, those verses of the psalm:

I will say of the Lord, He is my refuge and my fortress: my God; in him will I trust.

Surely he shall deliver thee from the snare of the fowler, and from the noisome pestilence.

He shall cover thee with his feathers, and under his wings shalt thou trust: his truth shall be thy shield and buckler.

Thou shalt not be afraid for the terror by night; nor for the arrow that flieth by day;

Nor for the pestilence that walketh in darkness; nor for the destruction that wasteth at noon-day.

He held us like men enchanted, not only by the tones of his voice, but also by his aspect, standing, with his hoary head and long beard, like an ancient prophet amid that sea-wilderness; and when he ended, we continued awhile silent and still. Even Obadiah was reached by the mighty song.

The first to speak was Mr. Vertembrex.

"The wind is rising," said he. "Let us set more sail, and run the hazard. Perhaps we shall outrun the leak. Do you not think, Kedgley, that we had better?"

The aged sailor simply nodded his head, and immediately after ascended the mast to set our main-course, being followed by Obadiah.

They were scarce gotten up, but we heard them crying to us as with one voice:

"A sail! A sail!"

"Why, we shall be saved, in spite of all!" said Mr. Vertembrex; and I said:

"It is like the words of the psalm come true!"

In the next moment, our ship swerved from her course, and, with a great shock of the waves upon her side, violently heeled.

Being overset, I was thrown into the scuppers. When I was able to recover my feet, supporting myself by the bulwarks, our ship was slowly righting, and Mr. Vertembrex, followed by Giles Kedgley and Obadiah (having let themselves summarily down from the mast) were running to the helm; where I beheld Mr. Huxtable fallen upon the deck, against the compass-stand.

I started off after them; and when I was come up, Kedgley and Obadiah were heaving on the tiller with all their force, and Mr. Vertembrex, kneeling down by his side, was observing Mr. Huxtable with an aspect of amazement.

"Sure it is nought!" cried I, casting myself down on the other side. "He is only stunned with knocking on the deck when the ship heeled."

"Nay," said he, "he was fallen before. The ship broached to because he left hold. I do think he is dying. Hush!"

While he spoke, I observed Mr. Huxtable's eyes, that were closed before, to open wide, shining with a sort of veiled lustre; and, in low tones, with such gentle, loving accents as fell like music on my ear, he said:

"Ay, Philip, the boy is much like you. I would you were able to behold him, as you do me."

And, a moment after:

"That's very like"; said he, "if you had known him in the world."

He spoke no more, and his eyes closed. They presently opened again; but he was dead.

Mr. Vertembrex was gone away; but there was no strength left in me to have risen up from the deck, where the labouring of our ship swayed me to and fro. Giles Kedgley spoke to me kindly while he stood steering, telling me that we were certainly descried, since that ship which he had seen, had altered her course to come to us. But, though I understood the sense of his words, the matter signified nothing to me; for, at the feverous approach of that distemper which long held me, I imagined that I was in the kitchen of Mr. Huxtable's farm while he uttered those affectionate words:

"If God send that I find my son, you two shall be as brothers."

For more Tales of the Weird titles
visit the British Library Shop (shop.bl.uk)

We welcome any suggestions, corrections or feedback you may have,
and will aim to respond to all items addressed to the following:

The Editor (Tales of the Weird), British Library Publishing,
The British Library, 96 Euston Road, London NW1 2DB

We also welcome enquiries through our Twitter account, @BL_Publishing.